The Gifts

The Gifts

Calesse Cardosi

Dear Taylor,
I hope you enjoy this! Remember
to keep reaching for your dreams
and doing what you love.

7/19/08

Love,
Calesse

HPH Publishing
Chicago, IL

Cover Illustration by Morgan Ramsdell, KoKo Mia Designs
Copyright: HPH Publishing Inc.

First printing 2007 (Publication date: September 29, 2007)

Publisher's Cataloging-in-Publication Data
Cardosi, Calesse, 1991-
  The Gifts / Calesse Cardosi.
    p. cm.
  ISBN–13 978-0-9776281-3-1 (alk. paper)
1. Heroes–Fiction. 2. Kidnapping–Fiction. 3. Fantasy.
I. Title.
  PZ7.C5918 2007
  [Fic]—dc22

20079255

To my parents,
Rich and Denise Cardosi

CONTENTS

Acknowledgements

I would like to thank my parents, first and foremost, for your loving and faithful support. They have been the most supportive parents a kid could ever ask for. No matter what my ambitions, be they silly or farfetched, they have always had my back, behind me one hundred percent of the time. I said I wanted to write a book? "Go for it!" they said with enthusiasm. They have also been the most influential figures in the development of the most important thing my life: faith in God; leading by example, they have shown me what it means to be a true Christian. Without both of you, I know I would not be the blessed, gifted, fortunate child that I am. Thanks for helping make this book happen. Oh, and Mom, thanks so much for driving me to my one million and one activities, cooking my meals, doing my laundry, along with every other wonderful thing you do day in and day out. Most of all, thanks for helping make this book happen. I love you both.

To Andrew, my loyal brother, thanks for all your support as well. I appreciate your patience with me and your willingness to put up with me day in and day out. You may never know how thankful I have always been just for having you around.

Marilyn Kramer, thank you so much for introducing me to Franchee Harmon, my dear patient publisher. You believed in me, a young inexperienced writer, and for that, I am forever in your debt. Franchee, thank you as well. Your careful revisions and insight into my writing has been extremely helpful.

Also, I would like to thank the many teachers I have had in the past, especially Mr. Campos, my 5th grade teacher and Mr. Billings, my 8th grade teacher. You have taught me so much of what I am tremendously grateful I know today. You are two of the really amazing teachers, of which there are far too few, who go out of their way to reach out to every individual student; the kind that leave a lasting impression on them for a lifetime. This book definitely would not be here without the help and faith these people have had in me. Thanks so much for your encouragement, the knowledge, and the skills you have given me. Also thanks to my awesome librarian from ACS, Athens who led an after school program where kids could write their own books. That was where I wrote my first piece of work, and she greatly inspired me, increasing my love for reading and writing.

Calesse Cardosi
May, 2007

The Gifts

I. Premonitions

"Mom, may I get a drink of water?" Jake whispered to his mother, who was staring at the preacher standing in the pulpit. She completely ignored her son as he squirmed around on the hard pew trying to find interest in the never-ending sermon. He tried to moisten his mouth to lick his chapped lips, but they were too parched. Turning to his tall, lanky father, Jake asked the same question and was rewarded with a response. Though it was not the most favorable reply, they were words nonetheless. This was nothing unusual. Jake and his younger sister, Amanda, were often disregarded and given little attention. They were not supposed to speak unless they were spoken to.

"No, son. Listen to Pastor Arnold. Shame on you for asking such a question! Pay attention, both of you!" Jake's father hissed, as Amanda's eyes wandered about the Cathedral. Her vibrant blue eyes had not dimmed despite five years of being ignored by her strict parents. They meandered from the stained glass window of Jesus on the cross to the Virgin Mary, and then to her father's menacing glare. Obediently, she folded her slender fingers in the lap of her only church dress, with its simple white lace design, and focused on the priest.

"But I-"

Their father's eyes quickly transformed into fierce red specks, blazing like a wildfire.

1

"I said no!"

Jake gulped, trying not to let the tears, welling up behind his eyelids, escape.

Zak awoke from his dream, tears stinging his sky-blue eyes. "What a terrible life! Who could survive such a horrific childhood? Oh well, it isn't real, only a dream—just a figment of my imagination." He snuggled up with his teddy bear and drifted off to sleep.

The next morning, Zak almost missed the school bus. He went sprinting down the street, waving his hands wildly and shouting at the top of his lungs, "Wait! Wait, I'm coming!" The other high school kids, already seated comfortably on the bus, snickered and pointed as he walked up the steps out of breath and looked around for a place to sit. But their laughter didn't ruin his day because Zak was naturally optimistic. He grinned as he scooted in next to his friend, Alex, and soon they began talking about last night's episode of their favorite TV show.

The scenery along the route to school added to the joy of the day. All along the suburban sidewalk, strategically planted trees seemed to dance as their leaves flowed with the breeze. Soon, the sun came peeking out over the horizon and shed a magnificent rosy glow on everything in the East. As he admired the view, Zak breathed in deeply, enjoying the start of another Friday.

Barking. Scratching. Barking. Snarling. Silence. Zak sat up

in his old oak bunk bed and smacked his head hard on a board from the bunk above.

"Ouch!" the boy moaned. He gently stroked his head, knowing a big purple bruise would be there in the morning. Sweat slowly streamed down his face, and his heart pounded as if he'd run a race. Panting, Zak laid back down and his blonde head sank deeply into his feather pillow.

"Why had that stupid dog next door been barking so loudly that it woke him up? And why was he drenched in sweat?" Then, it came to him. Another dream. Everything was so vague, wait. Wait … yes! It was coming back, like a thick fog clearing on a muggy summer's morning; images flooded his sleeping mind.

Zak walked cautiously down the three sets of marble stairs in his apartment building. Once outside, he turned the corner to the pitch-black side of the building. The dark shadows cast by trees blocking the glow of the street lamps were frightening. He quickened his pace as the shivering grass turned to cement beneath his bare feet. The walkway led right up to a seven-foot wall that separated his yard from that of the dog, Rex, and Mr. Coonfeld, his owner.

Mr. Coonfeld was a crotchety old man. Zak cringed at the thought of him. He could think of several negative encounters between them that he would rather forget. One evening, Zak had been playing with Ziad, the boy next door, and Ziad's brand new super ball had bounced into Coonfeld's yard. When

Zak and Ziad went to retrieve it, Rex violently tore the ball to shreds at Mr. Coonfeld's command. Furious, Ziad returned home and never spoke to Zak again.

Another time, Zak was collecting leaves for a school art project. Because his own yard had only a pine tree, which didn't shed leaves, Zak went to get fallen leaves from Coonfeld's. When Coonfeld discovered Zak, he exclaimed, "What are you doing, you foolish boy? Why are you stealing my leaves?! Those are good for the soil, makes it rich! Take your own leaves, not mine!"

"Sir," Zak began, "they're not all your leaves. They belong to everyone in your apartment building, and I really don't think it will hurt if I take a few leaves."

"Oh, we've got a smart aleck, do we? Be off with you, ya little whippersnapper. This world don't need the likes of you making trouble. Go on. Scat!"

"Yes, sir," Zak had said, and sadly returned home with nothing to complete his project.

"Pray for him, that's all I can do," Zak told himself. The poor old man was obviously deeply troubled to behave in such a disagreeable manner. Though he was slightly curious why Mr. Coonfeld was so unpleasant, at that moment, he didn't care to find out.

Zak approached the thick wall and examined it closely to figure out a sensible way to get over it. Several jagged metal poles stuck out of the smooth, concrete surface of the wall, and Zak found it odd that he had never noticed them before. Then again, he had never looked in detail at it before. Concluding that these would

serve well as hand and footholds, he'd scaled the wall within in a few moments. Swinging his limber body over the top, he landed skillfully, like a cat on the cool grass. Zak peered around at the dark, well-kept yard. There were silhouettes of many kinds of trees and shrubs in the darkness of the night. Timidly, he tiptoed over to the area beside the workbench, where Rex's cage was kept. A hammer, knife, screwdriver, and some rusty nails were scattered about. Rex's panting reached Zak's ears as he got closer. Nearly tripping on a fallen tree limb, he felt his way over to the heavy metal cage. Wait. He caught his breath at the sight before him. Scared to death, he shook his head and backed away. No, maybe he should do something. Zak had conflicting feelings pulling him in different directions. Shouldn't he call 911, the cops, fire department, his mom, someone? No, run away. The bloody mangled body was too horrifying. He knelt down hesitantly and reached for ...

"It was only a dream," sighed Zak. He rolled over and closed his eyes. Yet, all he saw was the body. Desolate, deserted and alone, cold, and mysterious.

Zak awoke to a garble of noise outside. Rubbing his eyes to prepare them for the morning light, a bit disoriented, he stretched his arms, glancing at the clock. Quickly, he bolted out of bed, for it was well past the time the school bus would arrive to pick him up. Suddenly, he remembered that it was Saturday. Sighing, he relaxed a bit. He stumbled out of his bunk and across the room to his window and peeked behind the navy blue curtain. The bright sunshine made him squint, and he had to wait a bit for his eyes to adjust. When the fuzziness cleared, Zak tried to figure out why there was a crowd outside Coonfeld's front gate. Three police cars, siren's whining and flashing red and blue, pulled up. Policemen placed yellow caution tape all around the perimeter of the apartment. They pushed the noisy crowd farther back. "What's going on?" thought Zak.

Zak awkwardly pulled on a pair of old blue jeans and an Earth Day T-shirt. He stepped into his scuffed-up sneakers and scrambled out of the apartment. "Be back by noon!" he yelled to his mom, who was reading a magazine at the kitchen table. As Zak approached Coonfeld's yard, he tapped one of the on-lookers and asked, "What happened?"

The man replied, "Dunno. Police showed up, and we got curious. Ya know, wanted to know what was goin' on."

"A lot of help that was," thought Zak.

"Thanks," Zak said and pushed his way further into the crowd towards a police officer. "Excuse me, sir. I live next door, in the apartment over there," pointing to his home. The officer nodded, raised his eyebrows, and waited for Zak to continue. "And, well, as a good neighbor, I was wondering what's going on and whether I could help."

"Well, thanks son," smiled the officer. "Perhaps you can. But I must warn you to brace yourself. This is a very serious situation." Zak nodded that he understood and dutifully followed the officer. The tall, slender policeman led him to the front of the crowd.

As Zak approached the gate, he tripped on a stone and struck his head on a low-hanging tree branch. Feeling like a klutz, awkwardly, he recovered and moved cautiously to the edge of the gate. Suddenly, he stopped. He could hardly believe his eyes. Seeing the color drain from Zak's face, Officer Coleman touched his shoulder and said, "Maybe this wasn't a good idea." Tenderly, he moved Zak away.

Zak walked slowly back to his apartment building. He knew he was awake, but the images were very clear in his mind. It was the same lifeless body from the dream the night before. And, the body was spread out in the dirt, eyes wide open, just like the dream. A look of pure terror and fright glossed them over like a transparent film of plastic. "How on earth could that be?" Zak questioned himself out loud. "It's not possible."

"Coincidence," said Mrs. Fredrickson calmly. It was two days later, on a bleary Monday morning. "A mere coincidence and nothing more. I wouldn't let it bother you."

"But mom, you don't understand!" pleaded Zak. "Everything was exactly the same as in my dream! There has to be something to this, a connection or ... something."

"Oh Zak, you've always had a lively imagination. But you are fourteen now—almost fifteen, for crying out loud—and I hate to be so blunt, but you need to grow up a little," Mrs. Fredrickson scolded.

"If dad were here, he'd take me seriously," spat Zak, frustrated.

Mrs. Fredrickson went frigid. "Don't speak of your father. He deserted us and doesn't deserve to be talked about." Mrs. Fredrickson took a sip from her steaming mug of morning tea. "You'd better get to school," she advised, glancing at her watch and scooting out of her chair. "Here's your lunch." She held a lumpy crumpled paper bag out to him. "Go on, you'll miss the bus."

Grudgingly, he accepted the lunch and shrugged his school

bag onto his back.

"Have a good day!" Somehow, she managed to sound cheery. Zak loathed when his mother tried to cover up problems. She swept them under the rug as if they never happened. It wasn't a good way to deal with issues, and it never worked. Like the divorce. Mrs. Fredrickson acted as if it had never occurred, and then when it popped up in conversation, as it inevitably and unavoidably did from time to time, she got all upset about it. Problems always sneaked up on them when they least expected it, and they ended up having to deal with them all over again! "Why not get it over with, talk it out, and solve the problem once and for all?" He thought in frustration, as he slumped out the door. Down the stairs he went and out to the bus stop. His friend Barry Hamilton was waiting eagerly for the bus that would take them to school, in his opinion, the best place on Earth. Most people called it a school bus, but Barry couldn't bear being normal. He called the school bus "the mystic vehicle of yellow, which takes us to the place where we fulfill our wildest yearnings."

"Hey, Barry," Zak greeted, sounding half-hearted.

"What's-a-matter?" Barry asked, concerned by Zak's dejected tone.

"Oh, uh, nothin' … just nervous about the English final, that's all," he explained, trying to cover up his real feelings. It was true. He was worried about the English final because he was teetering between a C-minus and a D. If he performed poorly on the exam, he was dead meat when his mom got hold of his grades.

"That all?" his friend asked suspiciously. Barry was one of Zak's closest friends and had known him too long to be thrown off that easily.

After a moment of hesitation, Zak decided to confide in his pal. "Not exactly. I've been having these weird dreams lately, and–,"

"You're worried about that?" Barry exclaimed, laughing. "Jeesh! Last night I dreamed I was a two-hundred-year-old tree in the rainforest. A group of tree-huggers was protecting me from a lumber company that wanted to chop me down! They held hands around me and sang wacky songs. Then one of the guys transformed into a bird and came to make a nest in my branches."

Just then Alex Thomson approached from around the corner and waved. "I see you got here on time today," he chided humorously.

Alex always looked like he was lost in thought. He was a talented writer with innovative ideas but often seemed to have his head in the clouds. Teachers frequently reprimanded him at school, and he constantly received poor grades because he never paid attention in class. As usual, when he reached the bus stop, he stuck his hands deep in his pockets, leaned against the bus stop pole, and gazed off into space.

Zak and Barry acknowledged him but continued their conversation. "Oh, that's very interesting." Zak murmured as the bus came to a jerky halt in front of the curb. Along with the other kids from Rolling Hills High, Zak and Barry climbed up the steps and onto the bus. Zak gave a smile to the bus driver and searched the crowded bus for a place to sit. "But this, this is different," he argued.

"How so?"

"The things in my dreams have actually … come true."

"Come on Zak, how can that be?"

"You're just like my mother!" Zak exclaimed in frustration.

Plopping down in a seat beside the window, Zak stared furiously at an overflowing dumpster, as the bus rumbled along.

Barry tried again. "I'm sorry, man. I shouldn't have said that. If your dreams are coming true, well … that's like good, isn't it?"

"No!"

"Why not?"

"Because," Zak shot back, "I dreamed about a dead guy, and it happened!" He said it so loudly that he got everyone's attention.

"What if by dreaming these things, it makes them take place?" Zak mused.

"Naaaa," Alex shot back. "It's the other way around. See," he began, gesturing for effect with his hands, "the things happen, and then you get … like …" He groped around for words. "Like a vision! You see things that go on. Your dreams don't make things happen, Zak. They simply happen, and for some reason, you can see them." Alex shook his head and went back to his own thoughts.

Leah Dixon, who was sitting several seats ahead, shook her glossy blond hair as if to make a point, then rolled her eyes dramatically. "I think you're all nuts, wacko, off your rockers!" she burst out. "You know what? You've been hangin' out with that one too long." She was pointing toward Alex, who chose to ignore her and continued gazing out the window. "Hel-ooooo," she sang, waving her hand. "Earth to Alex, Earth to Alex. Copy, do you read me?"

All the kids on the bus giggled as Alex was jerked from his daydream. He looked up suddenly, pointed out the window, and exclaimed, "That tree could be divided into fifty pieces and scattered to the winds, but it will always remain together in my mind. Things may change, but I will always know it for what it truly is."

Leah defiantly rolled her eyes, "Boys."

Later that night, dreading what he thought would happen, Zak sat up in his bed staring at the blackened room and the outlines of nightmare figures in it. Reluctantly, he drifted off to sleep.

Zak kneeled beside the old man. "That's Coonfeld all right," he said aloud, knowing there was no one there to hear him. Cautiously, he reached for the red leather collar clutched tightly in Coonfeld's cold, stiffened hand. After considerable effort, he pried it from his blue, lifeless fingers. Zak took out a flashlight and examined the collar. Printed in bold black letters was the name REX.

For once, the dog wasn't barking, which seemed unusual to Zak. Just as he paused to inspect Rex's collar in better lighting, two powerful, gloved hands covered his mouth. In the next moment, he was lifted off the ground. A burlap sack came swooshing down around him. "Aaaaah!" he screamed, but his cries were muffled and barely audible. "What are you doing? Let me go! I haven't done anything wrong!"

He felt himself swinging in midair. Through a peephole, he could see the ground rocking beneath him and a pair of shiny black army boots thumping swiftly forward. Kicking, punching, and protesting proved to be only an unwise use of energy. Soon, Zak went limp, listening and waiting.

Thump! "Ouch!" Zak clutched his left arm in agony. Shooting pain ran up and down the limb as if a needle had been stuck into him. "Where am I?" he asked himself angrily. He had landed on a hard surface, and his arm had broken his fall. Zak struggled out of the sack and found himself in the back of an old, beaten up van. Only seconds later, the motor started, and the tires made a screeching sound as the van lurched quickly forward, throwing Zak to the back of its cabin. Wincing from the pain, he attempted to move his arm but couldn't. "Crap!" he thought.

Zak awoke in a cold sweat, grabbing his left arm. "Another dream," he sighed to himself. "Or was it? Oh, I just don't know anymore!" He buried his head between his knees and tried to reassure himself that everything was under control, and he was safe. "All right," he admitted to himself, "it's been three nights. Now that's weird …" Zak felt disoriented and confused. He had no idea what was happening to him.

As bright sunlight slipped through the gaps in the curtains and shone on the Fredricksons' overstuffed couches and polished tables, there was a sharp knock, knock, knock at the door.

"Coming!" Mrs. Fredrickson sang merrily. She scuttled over to the freshly painted, crisp-white door, and opened it to the police officer from the Coonfeld crime scene.

"Good morning, ma'am," the officer greeted, removing his cap politely. "Officer Coleman's the name. This is my assistant, Officer Gere."

A woman officer stepped forward and stuck out her hand. "Pleasure to meet you, ma'am." The two shook hands cordially, and then Officer Coleman continued.

"We would like to have a word with your son regarding the death of a Mr … Um … ah wait–," He consulted his clipboard and said, "A Mr. Conner Coonfeld."

"Oh!" Mrs. Fredrickson exclaimed. "I was sorry to hear he had passed away. That's too bad. Oh! I seem to have forgotten my manners. Do come in."

The police officers smiled and stepped inside. "Would it be all right to have a word with your son?"

"I suppose that would be fine, but Zak is in bed at the moment. Would you like me to go and fetch him?"

"Yes, please do. What is your name?"

"Joanne Fredrickson."

"Ah yes," Officer Coleman said, nodding.

Mrs. Fredrickson stepped lightly down the narrow hallway leading to Zak's room and tapped softly on the closed door. There was no response, so she knocked again. "Zak, honey?" she whispered. No response. "You have visitors. You need to come out and greet them."

For a moment, she hesitated. When she still did not get a reply, she called a little louder, "Zak, wake up, dear!" Silence still. Finally, she turned the doorknob and stepped inside the dark room. Mrs. Fredrickson smiled as she walked over to coax her son from his cozy bed. "Come on out, Zak, there are police officers who have come to talk to you." She was about to plop down on the sea green bedspread when she noticed there was no lump under the covers. Alarmed, she threw the blankets back and saw that the bed was empty. "Oh my!" she gasped. "Officer Coleman! Zak's missing! Officer Gere!" Footsteps sounded on the polished linoleum as Officers Coleman and Gere ran towards Mrs. Fredrickson's voice. "He's gone!" she shrieked.

"Are you sure he's not in any other part of the house, like the rest room? Or watching television, perhaps?" said Officer Coleman calmly.

Frantically, Mrs. Fredrickson glanced at the bathroom. The door was slightly ajar, and Zak always closed it all the way. She rushed upstairs and poked her head in the TV room. Empty. The computer room, the office, the living and family rooms, the kitchen and the hall closet, all deserted and strangely empty, like an old abandoned mansion that kids dared each other to enter and explore. Finally, she went back to the living room, where the officers had gone to wait and take notes.

She entered the room and gasped, "He's gone, my baby's gone!"

"All right, all right, calm down, Mrs. Fredrickson. Your son is probably at a friend's house, or maybe the movies. Perhaps he went to the mall without telling you. Was there a fight or an incident the two of you had that might have motivated him to leave the house? Sometimes kids do that to make their parents sweat a little."

"No. Zak always tells me where he's going, and he never gets up before eleven on the weekends. We did have a small argument earlier in the week, but it was insignificant and stupid. Just an overactive imagination is all. It shouldn't have been an issue ..."

"But was it an issue?" Officer Coleman asked.

"Well, yes. I suppose it was."

"That could be your reason right there," Officer Coleman said assuredly.

"But I don't understand. How could he have gotten out without me seeing him? I've been right here in this kitchen, with a view of the front door since six o'clock this morning. It's just not possible."

"Well, I can't explain that right now Mrs. Fredrickson." He paused and cleared his throat nervously. She wanted desperately to understand what had happened to her son. "For now, we have a missing person."

"A missing person?" Mrs. Fredrickson asked quizzically.

"Yes, until we have more information, he is considered a missing person."

Mrs. Fredrickson sank into the love seat. She opened the drawer beside her, ignoring the scraping sound that normally drove her through the roof, and extracted a bottle of aspirin, extra strength. Opening the small plastic container, she took two out and swallowed them both.

Zak looked to the front of the motionless van. There seemed to be no one inside. Now he could escape! Crawling to the rear of the vehicle, careful not to put any weight on his injured limb, he flipped the lock and heard a satisfying "click." Swiftly, he placed his sweaty fingers on the door handle and jarred the door open slightly, but before he could alight from the vehicle, he heard the sound of heavy feet pounding on the pavement, running toward the van. Two men, one wearing the gleaming black boots from his dream, had come running to stop him. Placing his hand firmly on the door, the bigger one said, "What do you think you're doing, kid?" Zak said nothing.

"We're gonna have to teach him a lesson, ain't we Croogar?" said the one with the boots.

"Sure thing, Boss," sneered Croogar.

"Oh, no!" Zak thought. Fear gripped his heart like a cold

autumn wind.

"What do ya say, the cellar?"

"Sounds good, Boss. Come 'ere, ya lousy boy!"

Zak struggled as Croogar's calloused hands tugged at his sore arm. He even bit the man in a desperate attempt to get loose, but there was no response.

"Kid," Croogar cackled with glee, "I done this one hundred times over. Ain't nothin' you can do, no trick in the book that I ain't got pulled on me before. I is smart as a scientist when it comes to this!"

Well, that didn't change Zak's mind. He still tried to find a means of escape; he was simply not going to give up. His mind raced as he racked his brain for an idea. Zak weighed about 125 pounds, so he did not really have much physical leverage. There was no way he could topple the muscle macho! But Zak was a wrestler and a pretty good one at that, county champion three years running, and he played soccer, so he was quick on his feet, as well as agile. Thinking quickly, Zak decided to pull a wrestling move on the old geezer. Without warning, he swung one of his legs around Croogar's and used it as an anchor. The sudden movement caught Croogar off guard, and Zak managed to free himself.

Surprised, Croogar released his grip, and Zak was off like a gunshot headed for … well, he did not know exactly where; anywhere but here! He ran wildly, blindly in the darkness, hands outstretched.

Pow! Zak ran headlong into a cold cement wall. He was out like a burnt-out bulb. He flickered briefly and then fell to the floor.

Jake's eyes fluttered with exhaustion, for he had been reading the bible aloud to his sister from the time the family arrived home from church. The large oak grandfather clock hanging on the wall had just chimed five o'clock. He took great interest in reading a bible story or two, but when his parents forced him to read it for hours on end, it became tiresome.

"I hear the children outside," Amanda whispered, with a sad look of longing in her eyes. "I want to play with them." She quietly walked from the kitchen table to the large windows looking out onto the street. With a slight intake of breath, Amanda cried, "Oh! Look Jakey, they are playing baseball! I want to join them! Perhaps I could play second base, or outfield, anything." Jake went to his sister and laid his hands on her narrow shoulders.

"Come Amanda," he coaxed gently, as if trying to convince a cat to crawl out from under a bush. "Mother and Father will become angry if we don't continue reading. You know we're not allowed to associate with the non-believers. 'They will surely contaminate us with their pagan and heathen ways,'" he said, quoting his father in the same strict tone he used when talking to the children. "But you need not worry, God will get us out of here someday," he added sadly.

"I don't see what harm a half an hour of baseball with a few of the neighborhood kids would do, Jake. Why can't we go out there, Jake, just for a little while?"

He shook his head sadly. "You know we can't do that Amanda. Orders. Besides, we don't want to get punished. I still have marks on my back from last time. And being cooped up in our rooms for an entire day with no food and nothing to do was not fun either. Don't you remember?"

Amanda nodded. "Yes."

"Oh, I think I hear father and mother coming. Quick, back to reading!"

The two swiftly returned to the table, and with a lazy rubbing of his eyes, Jake continued to read the story of how Doubting Thomas fell into the water after trying to walk atop its surface as Jesus had done.

When Zak came to, he was bewildered and confused. "Who are those children?" he thought. Suddenly, he remembered crashing into the wall of cement. He could have gotten free if it weren't for that wall!

"Man! What a dream!" Zak said aloud. "Good thing it was only a …" Zak's words trailed off. "Are those bars?" he asked himself. Had his dream come true? Zak slapped himself once and then again. He walked over and kicked the wall with decent force. "Ouch! This is no dream: this is real!"

Looking around, there was nothing in his cell but some water on the floor. Not a tattered old bunk or cot, no toilet or primitive sink, just a single, dull, low-watt light bulb dangling precariously from a few wires on the ceiling. The rusty cell door was secured shut with a heavy-duty padlock, and there was no key in sight.

"Jeesh! What is happening to me?" Zak cried out in despair. He crawled over to a semi-dry corner of the cell. A hot tear trickled down his face, leaving a path along the dust coating his cheeks like a dried up riverbed. Then he cried. He broke down completely. Sobbing uncontrollably, Zak pulled his scratched and beaten knees up to his chest and wrapped his arms tightly around them, trying to hug himself. Then he screeched in pain amidst the searing tears filling his eyes. His arm! Zak cried until he couldn't produce any more tears. Thinking about his friends and family, he recalled the last thing he had said to his mother, which could, quite possibly, be the very last words she'd ever hear him say. That stupid fight. Why hadn't she believed him? It didn't matter much now … He was alone, with no one to care for him or comfort him or hold him tight in a warm embrace. He was alone in the blackness of the damp, cold cell. He drifted off into a restless sleep …

Now older, the two children sat at a long oak dining table, heads bowed in prayer.

"… and Heavenly Father, we thank you for this meal you hath given unto us. Guide us, oh Lord, to show us what we must do. Amen."

"Amen," the family muttered in response. They began to eat their dinner without a word. The father gave menacing glares to anyone who dared to look at him.

"I trust we all had a pleasant day," he said, trying to sound cheerful. Amanda, Jake, and Susan, the children's mother, nodded like zombies. Their vacant eyes showed no emotion as they shoveled spoonfuls of corn, peas, mashed potatoes, and beef into their mouths.

"We must do something!" cried Mrs. Fredrickson.

"Yes, we are doing our very best, ma'am. It's just that we need some way to identify your son." As the distraught woman looked helplessly at Officer Coleman, her eyes bore deeply into his heart. "A picture would prove quite helpful," he added.

"Oh, yes. I have one right here." Mrs. Fredrickson hastily snatched up a framed photograph from Zak's most recent school picture day and handed it to the officer. "Don't know why you didn't mention that earlier ..." she added in an undertone.

"Yes," he acknowledged. "This is the boy from the crime scene. I had forgotten what he looked like ... hmm. But yes, that's him. We really do need to find this boy. Everything is coming into place now, just like a jigsaw puzzle!" he exclaimed, excitement ringing in his voice. He mimed fitting pieces of a puzzle together in midair. "This may be a more serious situation than I had fathomed! The person who murdered Mr. Coonfeld could have abducted your son."

"My God!"

"Now don't you worry, Mrs. Fredrickson, we'll locate your son. You have to trust us."

Heavy footsteps echoed from a distance as Zak peered up from the floor of the cell. The black-gloved man appeared with the guy Zak had come to know as Croogar. "Boss" was clad in black: boots, gloves, leather jacket, cap, T-shirt, slacks. A burly man with a bristly beard, Croogar had impenetrable eyes and a steely gaze that sent shivers up and down Zak's spine. He appeared to be about fifty or sixty, yet still in excellent physical shape from the looks of his bulging muscles.

"Kid, we gonna take you on a boat ride, and you're going to enjoy it. But you make a sound, just one lil' peep–," Boss took his index finger and slid it across his throat. He uttered an unpleasant sucking sound, implying a knife slitting Zak's throat. "You're dead meat! You hear me boy?"

Zak nodded, for his throat was so dry with fear he couldn't speak. Croogar sunk his gnarled hand deep into the depths of his coat pocket and produced a key. He unlocked the cell door.

"Come 'ere!" he snarled. Zak was yanked forward and a rope was tied securely around his wrists. His arm was quite sore. An old blindfold that smelled oddly like mothballs and cologne was placed roughly around his fearful eyes. He was led—or shoved—through a series of hallways. Through a slit in the cloth, apparently unknown to his kidnappers, Zak could actually see what was going on and where he was going. He took in every minor detail, from the oak-paneled doors to the tapestries hung on the walls to the detailed and embroidered carpet and the white phone resting on a small table against the wall. "A phone … ? A phone!" he thought. "My key to the outside world! 9-1-1, police, the National Guard! FBI, mom, home, freedom!" Zak was just about to reach his hand out to snatch the ivory colored receiver off its cradle, but he held back, remembering his captors. They had no idea he could see through the blindfold. Perhaps he would get a chance to return to this place to call 9-1-1, but not now. Timing and planning were absolutely crucial right now. He couldn't waste what might be his one and only chance for escape.

To make sure Boss and Croogar thought he was blind, Zak stumbled on a wrinkle in the carpet that he saw perfectly well. "Ha! I fooled them!" he thought defiantly. To reinforce the illusion, Zak continued to trip and fall down the dim passageway, lit solely by fake torches. "Where am I anyway? In the basement of a medieval castle or something?" Zak's thoughts were interrupted as they nudged him up a steep set of stairs.

"Hey, Mister Croogar, sir, where are you taking me?" queried Zak.

"Can't tell ya kid."

"How come? Because I want to know. My mom says never, ever to go anywhere with a stranger, and I certainly don't know you or where you intend on taking me." Zak reached a landing at the top of the stairs and halted suddenly, breaking free from Croogar's grasp.

"You know me! I'm ... I'm yer uncle ... John! Croogar's my last name. You just don't remember me 'cause the last time I saw you, you was just this tall," Croogar held up his hand to just below his waist. "Er, not that you can see how tall I'm showin' ya, but you was somethin' like three years old."

Zak's mind was spinning. He wasn't really listening to a word the old man was saying. He was using the time to stall and figure some things out while he had the chance. "All right," he thought, "I'm not being held onto so all I have to do is get past Croogar ..." (who he knew for a fact was not his Uncle John because he did not have any uncles, just a half-sane old Aunt who he rarely saw) "... and get to the phone. Then I'll be home free!" Zak pretended to start walking with an unstable gait up the last flight of steps.

"That's right, keep movin'," Croogar growled. Suddenly, struggling free of the ropes that bound his hands and tearing off the handkerchief that veiled his face, Zak raced down all the stairs he had just come up. His feet pounded on the carpet as he swooshed by the many doors lining the hallway. It would be difficult, he knew, for Croogar to follow him unless he watched him run away, because further down the hallway, his footsteps were gratefully muffled by the carpet. He ran like he never knew he could run, and when he could no longer see Croogar's face, distorted with fury, he slipped quietly and smoothly into a room just off the main hallway.

He closed the door and slid his back against the heavy pine wood; he sank slowly to the floor and collapsed in a crumpled heap. Zak was panting from the chase, and he wished that his heart would stop pounding so hard, so he could become quieter. Footsteps. Zak was feeling slightly light-headed, but he held his breath despite the overwhelming urge to breathe and re-circulate oxygen to his brain.

"Where did that son of a gun run off to? He's got to be around here somewheres ..." Croogar muttered, his crackly voice piercing the silence of the room in which Zak sat hidden. Zak's lungs screamed for air. He sucked in one, slow, steady, risky breath and listened intently. Croogar's footsteps came dangerously close, and Zak could tell that he was approaching the door. "I'm not taking any chances; I have to find a better hiding place! Croogar is way too close for safety," he thought.

Zak stood up and walked to the far side of the room as quickly and soundlessly as possible. Peering behind a door set into the wall on the right side of the small room, Zak discovered a closet. "Hmm ... a closet ... which would be a very good hiding spot!" He stepped behind the door inside the cramped storage area and hid behind a long, button-down, wool coat that swept the ground as he pushed it aside so he could squeeze behind it. "Perfect! If Croogar does find this closet he'll never detect me behind this old jacket." Zak carefully pulled the door closed and strained his ears listening, trying with all his might not to move an inch or to rustle any of the dusty plastic coat covers.

The door burst open with a great swoosh of air.

"When I find you kid, mercy is gonna be the last thing

you'll get from me!" Croogar snarled angry, furious, outraged, and dangerous. His heavy boots clumped along the floorboards and creaked ever so slightly as he paced recklessly about the room. He came to a halt in front of the closet door and flung it open with such force he nearly wrenched it off its rusty hinges. Narrowing his eyes and breathing heavily, he searched among the numerous overcoats and gowns looking for the boy. When Croogar could not find Zak, who was crouching behind some shoeboxes hidden behind the long black jacket, he slammed the door in fury and stomped out of the room. The sound of Croogar's voice indistinctly grumbling to himself slowly faded, and after a short while, the echo of slamming doors disappeared. Zak sighed with immense relief. That was a close call, almost too close, and he was not looking forward to anything of a similar nature occurring in the near future. He would just have to play it safe without being so cautious that he would never escape from these men, whoever they were. A happy medium, that's what he needed to find … Zak then realized just how exhausted he was and decided it would not hurt to take a quick nap. The phone call to home could wait.

Stumbling out of the minuscule closet, Zak strode across the room to a twin bed, made up with sky-blue sheets and a patchwork quilt comforter. There were no signs of the room being occupied—other than the closet of garments—so Zak took off his shoes and snuggled under the cozy bedclothes. He closed his drooping eyelids and was sound asleep within minutes.

Zak awoke with a start. A puddle of moonlight was cast onto the wooden flooring through a crack in the shutters. Oh no, it was night! Zak had planned to take a quick nap, but it must have been hours! The glowing numbers on his watch flashed a quarter after midnight. Trying to prop himself up on his elbow, as he often did, Zak remembered his injured arm. "Eeeooow!" He groaned. Zak threw back the covers and made the bed in the moonlit bedroom. He smoothed out the wrinkles, ensuring the bed was exactly as he'd found it. Zak put his sneakers on and padded over to the window.

Sliding open the unlatched window was easy. Getting out of a two-story window was the slightly challenging bit, especially with Zak's extreme fear of heights. Sucking in a great lungful of cool night air, Zak gulped and began the painstaking descent, grasping the wooden siding for dear life. Slowly, so slowly it would have been difficult to tell if he was making any progress at all from the ground below, he moved one hand down, then the other, then one shaky foot, then the other. After a few minutes of this, he was about halfway to the prickly thorn bushes below. Zak moved his left arm carefully, but he put just a little too much weight on the injured limb. It gave way, and Zak slipped. Startled, he yelled out in fear, flailing in the air, desperately reaching out to cling onto something. He was falling, falling. Crash!

"Ooooo …" moaned Zak. He sunk deep within the prickly branches of a bunch of rose bushes. Struggling immensely, Zak worked his way out of the tangle of thorns and not-so-fragrant flowers. Well, now what? Home, he supposed. Zak tiptoed around the side of the building, which took him two minutes, and ran across the paved driveway.

Just as Zak was rounding the brick structure at a steady jog, huge calloused hands picked him up, stuffed him into the familiar burlap sack, and thrust him onto the carpeting of the same van. Oh no! Not again!

"Good work, Croogar my man. Off to the harbor!"

Once again, Zak was thrown to the back as the idling

engine started up and caused the van to speed rapidly forward. Croogar, who was driving, made a sharp turn, causing Zak to tumble to the left on his bad arm.

"Ouch!"

"Whas'a matter kid?" Croogar jerked his head back just long enough for Zak to understand there was a hint of worry behind the cover up look of loathing in the man's cold grey eyes.

"Nothing you'd care about, you sick, crazy creeps!" retorted Zak, infuriated at what these men were doing to him. "Just an injured arm!"

"Ooh, does the little boy want mommy to kiss it and make the pain go away?" Croogar asked in a mocking baby voice. Then he grumbled something about kids being such wimps these days. But when he glanced back again, Zak still noticed the worried flash in Croogar's empty eyes. It was quick, oh so brief, but Zak had not missed it. Was it just possible that he was a little worried for Zak's health?

Free of the sack, Zak could see better. Aside from the street lamps' luminous glow, the night was pitch black. Zak knew they must be nearing the harbor, because the tinkle of a ship's bell was audible, and beyond the tall street lights, the moon was reflected in the serene rolling of little waves—"wavelets," he liked to call them. The moon shimmered and danced, its reflection playing about the silhouettes of now-visible ships. For one brief and wonderful moment, Zak forgot where he was and who he was with and enjoyed the sight of the harbor. Then a great lurch of the van, flying over a speed bump, brought him back to his terrifying reality. It also threw him to the back of the van with such tremendous force that he tumbled right out of the moving vehicle, out the door whose latch had come undone from the excessive turbulence.

II. The Call

"Ma'am we can't continue our investigation until we inspect the crime scene … thoroughly." Officer Gere added, "And, well, not to put your hopes down but, truthfully, these things take time."

"Time, time … yes, of course. Do sit down. Can I get you anything to drink?"

"No, Mrs. Fredrickson. We've got to get to work."

"Ah yes. Work, work," Mrs. Fredrickson muttered distractedly, worrying about her son.

Officer Coleman stared with concern at Mrs. Fredrickson. The love seat she had collapsed into seemed to provide little comfort. She was sick with fear and anxiety.

"No drinks … must work … find son … these things take time … stay calm."

Mrs. Fredrickson stared blankly into space. Her once-vibrant, sea green eyes were dull with worry.

"We will be in Mr. Coonfeld's yard if you need us," said Officer Coleman, still concerned about the woman, another victim of a cruel act in an increasingly cruel world. "Don't hesitate to come get us if there's anything we can do for you."

"Zak, come home!" cried Mrs. Fredrickson. Officer Coleman turned away reluctantly and headed down the steps.

Mrs. Fredrickson turned to the table beside her and picked up the receiver of her telephone. She punched in some numbers and held the phone to her ear.

"Hi, Ed. It's me, Joanne."

"Joanne, I– I'm surprised to hear from you. I– Is it money you want, because I owe a lot of bills and–,"

Mrs. Fredrickson rolled her eyes in disgust as she cut him off. "No! I'm in trouble. Well actually, it's our son. He's missing, and I know you're still in Canada, but … I need you right now, Ed. Please come home." Mrs. Fredrickson felt a burning tear run slowly away. She collected herself and waited anxiously for his reply. There was a loud click on the other end of the phone.

"Ed? Ed! You can't abandon me again!" Mrs. Fredrickson stared at the phone as if doing that would bring back the deep voice of her ex-husband. She gently replaced the phone in its cradle as she felt her eyes brimming over with tears.

Zak shook his head to clear the blaring noise in his ears that came from the impact of his fall. He stroked his arm and tried not to bump it. Luckily, he had been able to roll into the fall and land on his right shoulder, which, although bruised, would recover in a few days.

Would his captors notice he'd fallen out of the van? Of course they would! The crashing sound it made when the back door flew open was deafening! But he could still escape.

Zak began running back to the mansion where he'd spent the night. Despite his urge to run in the opposite direction, he headed for the foreboding concrete building. There was a phone.

As Zak made his way across the dew-covered grass, he slipped and fell down. He tried to brush off the sticky wet grass covering his arms and legs. "Aw, man!" complained Zak, as if he didn't have enough on his plate right now!

Then, seemingly out of nowhere, a raspy voice whispered, "Kid, come here." Looking around, searching for the source of the mysterious voice, Zak stood up and walked toward a dark, squarish shape just ahead of him. As he got closer, he saw it was a cardboard box in the shelter of a large and noble tree that stretched into the blackness of the star-speckled sky.

"Hhh-hello?" stuttered Zak, rather cautiously.

"Come here!" repeated the voice with an edge of agitation. Zak walked around the side of the grimy box and peered into a pair of emerald-green eyes.

"Kid, you got any money?" a hobo asked. There was a pleading tone in the man's voice.

"Uh … no sir, I don't have any I can spare at the moment. Sorry, how about a rain check?" Zak laughed at his own cleverness because he knew perfectly well he would never see this pathetic excuse of a guy again in his life. But it was a multi-faceted laugh, too. For if the man was not a dimwit, as Zak had assumed, he'd be in a fix, because then he would see Zak was trying to take advantage of him. Anyway, what was he playing at, trying to be mean to a homeless guy? That wasn't what Jesus would do, was it? Oftentimes, Zak had to make a conscious effort to question his own actions and make sure he was doing what God wanted him to do and not to listen to the devil, always trying to pry into his mind and control his actions. The hobo groaned and scowled. It was apparent that he was immensely displeased.

"Come on, boy. Five bucks?"

"Oh all right, but use it wisely. Don't go wasting it all on drugs or alcohol, you hear?"

The genuine smile on the man's face told Zak all he needed to know. It told him the man's intentions for the money; commentary and explanation were not necessary.

"Of course! What do you think I am, some kind of common criminal?" The man sounded rather disappointed at Zak's preconception of his character. "I'm saving up to rent an apartment with a few of my pals. Gonna go to community college and get a job too." He seemed quite proud of himself, so Zak commended him on his efforts.

"Well, good for you. Good luck with all that," he commented as he removed a crumpled-up five dollar bill from his pants pocket and held it out to the man. The hobo received the donation with supplication and tucked it carefully away. Then he motioned for Zak to sit down beside him. Zak was a bit hesitant, this guy being a total stranger and a homeless one at that, but he crawled inside the mildew-covered and cramped hut despite his feelings.

"So, tell me, boy, what's yer name and watcha' doin out this time o' the night 'round these parts, eh?"

"Well, the name's Zak, and I was kidnapped from my home in San Francisco by two men. One of the men's names is Croogar, and I don't know who the other guy is. Croogar refers to him as 'Boss.' It all started with this dream I had one night ..." Zak relayed the entire story from start to finish. He told this man he hardly knew all the details, his thoughts and feelings, without a second thought. "And now I really, really need to be going 'cause I gotta find a phone to call home."

The hobo's name turned out to be Chester, and he was left

out on the streets because his wife divorced him, withdrew all their money from the bank, and disappeared, never to be heard from again. The woman was an accountant, but Chester had dropped out of high school at the age of fifteen because he had to run the household when his father died of a drug overdose. So Chester had no college or completed high school education to draw on to get a job.

"But I've become acclimated to life on the streets. It ain't so bad … after you get used to it, that is …" A smile that warmed Zak's heart spread from the man's creased and crinkled eyes to the corners of his wrinkled mouth, which was filled with a whole bunch of yellowing teeth that gleamed in the dim light. His smile seemed to illuminate the hut with its brilliance, as it stretched across the entire width of his gaunt and bearded face. Chester did the best with what he had and had plans to improve upon the poor situation he was dumped in against his will.

"I'm truly grateful for yer money, but more so for yer time. Ain't nobody ever came in here and sat an' a-talked with me. I truly appreciate it, my young lad. I pledge to spend your money wisely."

"Good," Zak said as he stood up to leave. His mind wandered to more pressing matters, as he waved goodbye to his newfound chum. Now … to the phone!

Mrs. Fredrickson's telephone rang with a shrill tone. Brring! Brring! Brrrrr- She cut off the third ring as she snatched up the receiver and held it to her ear.

"Hello?" There was deadly silence on the other end. "Hello?

Speaking …"

"J– joanne?"

"Yeah, it's me …"

The deep, masculine voice on the other end let out a loud sigh of relief.

"I'm sorry for hanging up on you earlier. I booked a flight to San Fran tonight, and I'm flying in tomorrow morning."

"Oh Ed! I'm so glad you decided to come! I really need you right now … for moral support and everything!" She gushed.

"Yeah, well I'm doing this for our little Zakkie. Not for you. I want to make that quite clear, Joanne."

"Oh, well, you haven't changed a bit, now have you, Ed?" Mrs. Fredrickson spat, the words slipping out of her mouth like nasty bile.

"Whoa! Back off tiger! Nor you. You're still the same old feisty woman I left."

"I don't like change," she replied smugly.

"Yes, well I expect you will have a taxi waiting for me when I arrive at the airport?"

"I most certainly will not! Arrange it yourself!" Mrs. Fredrickson responded, incensed by her ex-husband's nerve.

"All right, all right," Mr. Fredrickson sounded flustered. "I'll see you tomorrow then."

"I don't look forward to it, but I'm still happy that you are coming."

"For Zak," Mr. Fredrickson added to reinforce his purpose for flying all the way from Toronto.

"Yes of course, for Zak!" Mrs. Fredrickson shouted, rather annoyed. Then they both hung up. They both sighed. They both wished that they could make their relationship work, if it was only to benefit their son. And, deep within their hearts, they both knew it couldn't work. Wouldn't work and never would. It was like two pieces of a puzzle that don't go together: no matter how many times you try to force them to fit or how many different ways you turn them on a different angle, they just won't slide into place like all the other pieces.

Officers Coleman and Gere came bounding up the immaculately polished marble stairs and burst eagerly through the door. The two were panting and out of breath, but they had a look in their eyes like they had something very important to share. Mrs. Fredrickson, looking startled, probed, "What is it?"

"Oh Mrs. Fredrickson! Spectacular news! We've found evidence that can get us started on determining where your son went off to." Officer Coleman smiled triumphantly, his face glowing with pride, and he took a seat on the coffee table directly in front of the troubled mother who hunched over on the love seat, elbows resting on her knees.

"Well?" Mrs. Fredrickson asked anxiously. "What did you find out?"

"All right. Coonfeld's dog, Rex, started barking and whining a lot when we gave him a shirt of Zak's to get his scent. Also, what really puzzled us was that there were two identical collars with the name 'Rex' inscribed on them. There were large boot footprints in the soil of Coonfeld's undeveloped area of the garden, and we found fibers stuck in a particular patch of grass near Rex's cage. The fibers, upon closer inspection proved to be from a potato sack."

Coleman paused, mulling over this perplexing and newfound information. Officer Gere piped up, "We also discovered some skid marks on the main road behind Coonfeld's apartment building. We called for assistance and Detectives Randal and Coovet are on their way." The two officers were beside themselves with joy and excitement. Never before in their careers had they had such definitive leads as this, such a trail to follow!

"Thank you very much for your assistance. I'm very glad you could help me," Mrs. Fredrickson praised them with gratitude.

"Why, it's our job. I'm afraid our work has only just begun. Now this information leads us to believe that there is an extremely high probability that your son has been kidnapped and that it has something to do with Coonfeld's death," Officer Coleman continued. "We do not have all the details yet, but we are making significant progress. Now we need to trace any and all phone calls you receive because the kidnappers may call for a ransom."

Officer Gere added, "Your son might attempt to contact you to tell you where he is, if he gets a chance, of course."

Mrs. Fredrickson nodded her head in agreement. "Do whatever is necessary. I just want my Zakkie home!"

Zak jogged across the grass, made a left turn onto the sidewalk, then another left, and the enormous building, he was dreading so much, came into view. He stopped behind a cluster of shrubs facing the building and crouched low to the ground. He gulped. "Do I really want to go back there?" Zak asked himself, now doubting his plan, but he knew it wasn't a matter of whether or not he wanted to return, it was a matter of necessity. He had to go back, no matter how terrified he was of the place. Zak knew darn well that was exactly what he had to do. He took a deep breath to build up his courage and rose up to a standing position, all the while staying alert and watching for lurking figures in the darkness.

Zak set out onto the lawn. He looked in every direction, squinting to see if anyone, or anything, for that matter, was watching him, perhaps from inside the protective shroud of fog that hung eerily about the courtyard. There was nobody in sight, only a stray cat that stared suspiciously from a few yards away, eyes narrowed to menacing slits.

"Shoo!" Zak scolded with a stage whisper. The striped cat remained motionless, so he began to nudge it with his foot. It hissed—the noise piercing the silence—gave Zak a final look of discontent, and scampered off.

Zak hated cats, despised them, loathed them, and detested them. They were too independent. "What good was it to have a pet that you wanted to frolic and play with if all the creature wants to do is walk around like it's the king of the world? All they do is lick themselves and then cough up nasty fur balls all over the upholstery, which they claw to shreds!" he thought in disgust. "Well, at least the thing was gone now."

Shadows in slow motion and beams of light cast from unknown sources played about the grass. Zak crept across to the large red door in the distance, cautious, nerves on end as if he was trying to escape from prison. A blinding floodlight could be pointed on him at any moment, or so it seemed, so he scampered around like a squirrel. Try as he might to remain inconspicuous and silent, Zak kept stepping on dead leaves and fallen twigs. Every time that happened, Zak would freeze in mid-step, look all around, listen, sigh with relief, and continue on, clutching his heart from the scare.

The boy slid inside the red-painted door. Now that his eyes were fully adjusted to the darkness, he could see that he was in the hallway he had been pushed through earlier. The flaming torches were extinguished (probably dimmed with the flick of a light switch), and he saw the phone right across the hall. He walked swiftly over and picked it up. Zak dialed his home phone number and waited in anticipation.

Officer Coleman sat patiently next to Mrs. Fredrickson, studying his notes from Mr. Coonfeld's yard, which were scrawled messily in a spiral bound notebook. Mrs. Fredrickson drummed her neatly manicured fingertips in a repeated, humdrum pattern on the edge of the coffee table. All they could do was wait. Zak's mother wouldn't let her gaze stray from the phone, acting as if, if she looked elsewhere the phone would never ring.

Brring! Mrs. Fredrickson glanced at Officer Coleman who stared at her. "Answer it!" demanded the man sternly.

"Oh, right." She picked up the phone nervously and held it to her ear as steadily as possible for her hands shook nervously, making the jewelry on her thin wrists jingle softly.

"Hello?"

"Mom? It's me, Zak."

"Honey, where are you?" Officer Coleman tapped something into his laptop, and within moments, the map of a small town in San Diego near the coast popped up, and a red blinking light appeared.

"Mrs. Fredrickson, he's in San Diego," he informed her in a whisper-ish kind of tone.

"Mom, I miss you–,"

"Ohhhh!" she shrieked, covering her mouth with one hand. "Zakkie? Honey are you there?"

"What is it?" Officer Coleman queried, his voice edged with sincere concern. He rose slowly to his feet, setting his laptop aside.

"There was a muffled sound, 1– like struggling ... I don't know and then he wasn't there anymore, he didn't answer ... I don't know what it was ... what happened ..." whispered Mrs. Fredrickson as her voice trailed off.

"Oh boy," sighed the police officer, running his hands through his wavy, chestnut-colored hair.

"Let go of me!" ordered Zak, struggling to free himself from Croogar's tight grasp.

"Oh no, sonny. Not this time," Croogar cackled as he forced Zak's boney wrists into a pair of handcuffs. The key to his restraints was jingling loosely from a chain around the old man's neck.

"R'member that boat ride I was tellin' ya about? Well it's still on, and that is where we're headed! And no funny business this time, ok?"

"No!" Zak screamed defiantly. But soon he discovered, with a sinking feeling in his heart, that it was impossible to get loose.

Down the dimly lit hallway the two men walked once again; up the stairs and out the heavy metal door leading onto the street. Stars twinkled their last lights for the night. Dawn was quickly creeping up on the world. Soon, it would begin extinguishing the remaining stars, leaving a soft pink sky glowing with radiance from heaven.

"Pick it up, Croogar," Boss said anxiously glancing at

his Rolex wristwatch. "It's almost five o'clock, and we got a schedule to stick to. We ain't at the harbor yet! This rascal's cost us enough precious time already."

"Yes, Boss. Get in, kid," Croogar ordered, looking flustered and distracted. Zak crawled into the back seat of the van, careful not to put any weight on his bad arm, and sat down. The motor started up and roared like an irate fire-breathing dragon, as Croogar inserted the key into the ignition and turned it. While the engine was humming as it warmed up, Boss scolded loudly, "Dang-it, Croogar! Ya forgot to buy the muffler again! I'll tell you what that shows me: irr-es-pons-i-bility!" He drew out the last word with great emphasis. It was dripping with the disgust Boss felt for Croogar for being so lackadaisical about his job, his duty.

"Sorry, Boss. I reckon it won't happen again." Croogar averted his eyes, sheepishly fiddling with a lose thread on his shirt.

"You reckon? You reckon?! You will assure me it will get done!" he spat, lips spattered with flecks of spit.

"I assure you, I will go and get it Boss, no doubt about that. An' it won' happen again," he replied looking down in shame and embarrassment. Zak was sickened by the way Boss treated his assistant; it was absolutely repulsive, but he didn't dare say a thing for fear he might suffer the brunt of the blow for sticking up for somebody in front of such a power-hungry monster.

"No, it won't!" Boss stared at his crony, who in his eyes was pathetic and trivial, insignificant and worthless, with a steely gaze. But Croogar timidly looked away.

"Who on Earth would have the slightest inclination to work for such a terrible, abusive guy like that?" Zak wondered, dumbfounded. Then, he thought again. "Perhaps he didn't have a choice …" That thought saddened him.

About twenty minutes later, after a jolting ride of hairpin turns and abrupt stops, the van came to a screeching halt.

"Croogar, take the kid. I'll go hide the van," Boss ordered sharply. Croogar nodded in agreement. "I have a name!" Zak thought, maddened by the fact that they refused to inquire as to what it was and continued to refer to him as "the kid." "Besides, what does that cave man talk mean anyway? 'Take kid, I hide van.' Well, take kid where, hide car where?" Zak had little time to ponder these thoughts, for Croogar had hopped down from the passenger's side of the vehicle and gone around the passenger side to get him.

"Come with me," growled the balding man. Zak obediently stepped down from the van and was pulled roughly, as was Croogar's customary way of hauling him around, toward the dock.

"So, uh … where are we going?" asked Zak, naturally a tad bit worried.

"Oh, you'll see, you'll see."

Zak frowned. "It must be pretty horrible if they refuse to tell me!" he thought in a panic.

The two walked across the grassy park toward the harbor, Croogar towed Zak, who struggled to remain upright as he walked behind him. They stumbled onto the decaying pier with boards missing every few steps. The dock looked rickety, unstable, and untrustworthy, and Zak worried that the rotting wood could not support the weight of the three men once Boss arrived. He feared they might fall through what was left of the dock and go crashing into the sea. Hands bound together, Zak would surely sink. Just the thought of drowning here was enough to make him shiver violently.

Croogar hastily walked onto the gangplank leading onto a fair-sized motorboat. Zak eyed the boat suspiciously and with great scrutiny. The cracked windshield was covered with a thin, filmy layer of salt from waves that had come spilling over the sides of the craft. The boat, apparently named *The Adventurer* from the peeling words on the side of the haul just above the water line, was slippery, grimy, and looked sufficiently unstable and unfit for sea.

"What are you waitin' for? We ain't got all day!" Croogar snarled impatiently.

"N-nothing," Zak stammered. "But, are you sure this thing is ..." he looked over the boat another time, "seaworthy?" Croogar grunted and turned his back. So Zak boarded the craft and looked to Croogar for a hint as to what was going on.

"Go below deck and scrub the windows 'till all the grime and what not's disappeared. Then when yer through, I reckon you can mop this here filthy deck. Supplies is in the closet, first door on yer left." As Zak stared blankly at the old man, he instantly became visibly annoyed. "Get a move on it!"

Croogar unbound his hands, and Zak scrambled down the narrow staircase and got to work right away. The boy wasn't used to manual labor, but he had watched his mom clean before, how hard could it possibly be? Twenty minutes later, Zak had finished the windows. They were shined so well you could see your reflection staring back at you, and if you looked beyond yourself, you could see the wavering water swaying up and down with the slow rhythmic movement of the current. Clambering up the steps, Zak surveyed the salt-spewed deck and headed for the supply closet to fetch a mop.

Boss stumbled aboard with a clearly displeased attitude and barked like a drill sergeant in the Army, "Croogar! Start the engine and head for Quaqilé Island!"

"Yes, Cap'n."

"And don't call me captain!"

"Yes, Ca–, I mean Boss." Boss stomped downstairs in a huff while Croogar prepared to depart from the dock. He put the craft into gear and slowly backed out of the harbor, motor bubbling and leaving a path of white foam trailing behind. As soon as he cleared the other similar looking run-down boats and was more or less in open water, he eased the throttle forward until *The Adventurer* was slicing through the water at tremendous speed. Zak gazed at Croogar as he made slight adjustments to the boat's course and speed. Every now and then, a light would flash and he would press a button, twist a dial, pull a knob, or flick a switch on the panel beside the throttle and steering wheel.

"So, Quaqilé Island? That's where we're headed?" Zak asked. Croogar's response was an indistinguishable grunt and slight nodding of the head. "Oh, I see," Zak muttered sarcastically, as if those gestures really had answered his question. As he mopped up the grime encrusting the ship, he stepped over a damp cardboard box and an abandoned checkers game, some of the pieces lying at the bottom of the sea no doubt, and made his way over to the stern of the small craft. Zak had a disturbing, unsettling feeling in the pit of his empty stomach that these questionable characters did not have his best interest in mind. But how could he escape a boat that was getting further and further away from land with every passing minute?

III. The Island

"Well, what are we waiting for?" queried Mrs. Fredrickson impatiently. Officer Coleman was becoming agitated and turned to Officer Gere so that she could calm the woman down; he simply did not have the energy to do it himself, for his patience was wearing thin.

"Mrs. Fredrickson," began Officer Gere, "you need to try to work with us here. We are doing the very best we can. We have telephone tracings set up, back-up police in place, detectives investigating the crime scene–,"

"Yes, I know. I apologize. It's just that ..."

"I understand." Officer Gere gazed at her with empathy and compassion, trying to force a smile. Although she didn't let on, the future was looking dim for the woman's son, whom she desired so much to cuddle, safe and sound in a motherly embrace.

"Actually," Officer Coleman interjected, "I have arranged for us to fly into San Diego after Mr. Fredrickson arrives."

"Wonderful!" Mrs. Fredrickson's face lit up with hope. "But–,"

A loud, sharp knocking was heard. Everyone's heads jerked

towards the front door. Outside on the landing, leading off the staircase, a man uneasily shuffled his feet, clad in shiny patent leather shoes. He squinted at the crumpled piece of paper in his sweaty hand. "Yes, this was is correct apartment number … Perhaps, she wasn't home," the man thought as he waited.

Mrs. Fredrickson paused with her hand hovering above the shiny brass doorknob. She glanced back at both police officers for support as she nervously bit her lip. Finally, the door was flung open. The two stared blankly at one another.

"Er … uh …" Mr. Fredrickson didn't quite know what to say or how to say it.

"Oh, come in."

Mr. Fredrickson nodded apprehensively and stepped over the threshold. Officer Gere arose from her perch on the couch to introduce herself.

"Hello, my name is Officer Gere. This is my partner, Officer Coleman. Pleased to meet you, sir."

"Mr. Fredrickson," was all the man said, as he eyed the woman warily. Officer Gere was rather taken aback by his abruptness but quickly recovered and got right down to business.

"As you know your son has gone missing, but we got a call from him and traced it coming from a coastal area … ah … in San Diego."

Mr. Fredrickson helped himself to a chair and swiveled it backwards so it was facing the group. Straddling the seat with a leg on either side of the chair, he sat down. He was wearing brown slacks, a blue and white striped collared shirt, and loafers. Perched low were a pair of wire-rimmed glasses, which he pushed further up the bridge of his stately nose with his index finger. His shaven head glistened like freshly polished silverware in the early morning sunlight and his beard, though rather lengthy, was neatly trimmed and groomed. Mr. Fredrickson set his suitcase down, which had been balanced precariously on the edge of his knee, and clasped his hands together.

"Well, let's go." Mr. Fredrickson rubbed his hands, eyes eager with anticipation.

"Sure. You're ready to leave now? All ready? But you have just arrived, you just got here!" exclaimed Mrs. Fredrickson.

"Yes, I know that, but I want to find my son now. Who knows what could be happening to Zak at this very moment?"

She shuddered and nodded knowingly. "Just let me get my suitcase." She hurried up the stairs and returned a moment later, bag in hand.

"All right, the flight leaves at one p.m., and it's half past ten right now so we've got ample time. Traffic might delay us though ..." Officer Gere paused to take inventory of her things and to make sure everything—note pad, pen, cell phone, walkie-talkie, and bag—was with her and packed them up. "So we'd better leave soon," Officer Gere continued.

"Let's go!" Mr. Fredrickson cried with great enthusiasm, which was very uncharacteristic of him, as he snatched up his luggage and held the door open for the others.

Zak leaned against the railing on the edge of the boat and gazed out across the ocean. The surf pounded against the algae-covered haul and sent flecks of salty spray onto the deck. "God," he prayed silently, "watch over my mother. If I don't survive this crazy escapade, please do not let her worry too much. I put my trust in your hands, Lord, so please protect me." Zak went below deck and stood before the Boss who was watching the waves crash and foam against *The Adventurer*, as if mesmerized by its tranquil repetitiveness.

"What do ya want now?" asked Boss grumpily, pronouncing the now as if Zak had asked for a million other things in the past five minutes.

"Well, er, I uh … I've not eaten for two days sir, and well …" he rubbed his empty stomach and tried to swallow down his intensifying hunger. "I was wondering if I could have something … anything to eat."

"Hmmmm … we are going to do away with you anyway, why do you need food?"

Zak gulped and licked his lips, trying to grope around in his mind for some witty response.

"If you want me to die of starvation before you can kill me, or whatever it is you plan to do with me, that's up to you."

The Boss took that into consideration and stroked his stubbly chin. "I suppose it couldn't hurt," he mumbled aloud, turning over the idea in his head.

Relief swept over Zak like a cool autumn breeze, and a smile spread across his gaunt and rapidly thinning face. "Go to the cabinet over there and scrounge around, you should be able to find something edible in there. Oh, and there are also a few things in the refrigerator." The Boss pointed behind him with a lazy gesture of his hand, all the while his cold eyes never straying from the continual rolling and explosion of the waves.

Zak practically ran to the cupboard and threw open the doors. His eyes feasting on the goodies within, he snatched an extra large bag of potato chips, a box of raisins, a liter of grape soda, some pretzels, a half eaten loaf of bread, two Hershey's chocolate bars (one milk chocolate and one with almonds), and a bag of half-eaten jelly beans. He scampered over to the refrigerator and extracted an apple, some cheese, a chicken breast, and some mashed potatoes. Spreading the magnificent banquet out on the table in front of him, he spent only a moment gazing at it, like a miser stares at money in pure greed and fascination, before he could hold himself back no longer and dug into the food. When he had eaten until he was sure his stomach would surely burst, and he was fully contented, he forced himself up the steep set of stairs and rested on the upper deck.

The sun was now fully visible among several wispy clouds that hung low in the sky like lazy seagulls riding the warm air currents. Zak shielded his eyes with his hand and tried to get a glimpse of a dark line, a shadow, a bird, something to tell him that land was near. All he saw was a lightly colored patch of water in the distance and what looked like some small pointy things protruding from the water. They were not fully submerged as the remainder of the structure was. "Hmm … wonder what that is?" Zak mused. Upon closer inspection and as the ship approached the mysterious thing, Zak saw it was a coral reef. And they were going to drive right over it! Zak opened his mouth to holler to Croogar when all of a sudden a loud scraping sound was heard. The rough sound of rock on metal pierced the monotonous purr of waves lapping at the sides of the boat and split the early morning placidness. The rumbling sound bored right through Zak. He cringed as the boat shook violently. He steadied himself by griping firmly onto the corroding metal hand railing. They came to a halt: a complete standstill in the slowly waving motion of the crystal clear water.

"Croogar!" Boss appeared from the small doorway leading

to the cabin on the lower deck. He was absolutely furious and his face was swiftly changing to a purplish red shade as a result of his rage. "What have you done?!" Why's the boat stopped? We're wasting valuable time here, precious time that we'll never be able to gain back!"

"I– I … I don't know. All of a sudden …" he stuttered uncontrollably as Boss pinned him down with a fierce, powerful gaze. Zak interjected, a tad annoyed himself at Croogar's failure to notice the reef.

"I'll tell you what happened. What happened was, we ran into a reef!" Zak shouted angrily, his own face tingeing slightly red.

"What should I do Boss?" Croogar asked timidly, almost as if he were afraid to do so. Boss squinted, looking out onto the open water.

"I see Quaqilé Island; it's not too far away from here, maybe a mile or so. We'll have Justin come tow us in, if he's not completely wasted that is. Gimme the radio." Boss stuck out his hand, as he glanced at Croogar who was frantically rummaging around in a drawer beside the steering wheel. When he withdrew the radio from the pile of miscellaneous objects strewn inside the drawer, Boss snatched it out of his quivering hand.

"Justin, come in Justin?" Boss waited silently. "Justin, you perpetually drunken fool, pick up the confounded radio!"

There was fuzziness coming through on the other end, but then a sluggish and slurred voice replied, "Eh, what's that blasted noise, grrrrrr … I'm tryin' to sleep …" But the rest was indistinguishable. Then Justin must have located the radio because he growled, "Who's this?"

"It's yer Boss, and I'll have yer job if you don't come out here right now to Coral Rough and tow us in pronto. We've been grounded, so make it snappy!"

"Yes sir! Right away, sir!" There was a click on the other end so Boss turned the dial on his radio to "off."

It was quite obvious that, by this time, Boss was mad. No, not mad, extremely angry, infuriated would suit the situation better.

"Well?!" Boss growled expectantly. "What are you waiting for? The seasons to change? The world to end? Me to get any more tolerant or kind? You should be down there in the haul trying to repair that great gash in our ship's side."

"Yes, sir. Of course, sir." Without dawdling or wasting time, Croogar disappeared and in no time at all there was much banging and noisy racket. Boss stared out at the island and huffed impatiently.

"Where is that good for nothing Justin?" he muttered as he glanced briefly at his polished Rolex watch and looked out across the water again.

After a while, Croogar reappeared with, a hammer in his gnarled hands, sweat ringing his armpits and streaking his dirty face. "Good man, Croogar."

"Well, actually, Boss, you know I tried real hard 'n all but …" his gaze drifted from Boss's accustomed judgmental glare and rested on a large bloody scrape that ran all along his arm.

"And?" probed the Boss.

"I jest couldn't fix it. Think she's beyond my caliber of repair, sir. An' we's sinkin' fast. I's sorry."

"Croogar, you useless–," Just then, Boss stopped in mid sentence as all three heads turned at the sound of a whining motor. A drunken and jolly man, rather like Santa Claus—minus the beard—waved from a motorboat about half the size of the vessel the men were currently on.

"Justin!" Boss cried in relief as the boat pulled up along side *The Adventurer.* "Where were you?"

"Oh," Justin chortled, "sorry Boss. Had a little too much to drink las' night. Please, I beg your pardon. Ya know how it is with the drink and me. She loves me almost as much as I love her." He chuckled and smiled revealing teeth; some chipped and brown around the edges and others missing. Justin's trousers were thoroughly caked in dirt and his shirt, about the same level when it came to cleanliness, was in great need of patching. His thick mop of gray hair sat above his face shining with sweat on his very round head and wavered lightly as a weak gust of wind blew by. "I'll bring yees all ashore and send Scrubs to tow in *The Adventurer.* Sound good to you, Boss?"

"Scrubs?" Boss asked, raising his eyebrows in befuddlement. "Who's that?"

"Oh, you know, the new hired boy. Don't speak much, but he's good fer doin' work." He thought a minute, shrugged, and then added, "Maybe he just don't got much to say."

"Shall we board then?" Boss asked sarcastically.

"Certainly sir."

Zak got on first. He put one leg over the waist-high railing and then the other. Then he climbed down a length of rope hanging from the rail. Once he was onboard, Boss and Croogar followed suit, stumbling aboard in a very awkward way.

"Get going, Justin. We haven't got all day!" Boss ordered instantly. Clumsily, Justin started up the engine and headed full speed for a rickety looking wooden wharf a little ways in the distance amidst the swiftly lifting fog.

Hardly shy by now, Zak stuck out his hand and politely introduced himself. "Hi, I'm Zak. You're Justin, I presume. So, what's your job with this whole kidnapping deal? You can tell me, don't be scared." Speechless and shocked, Justin gave the bold boy an astonished look. "Aw, come on, please?" Zak pleaded.

"I suppose ..." Justin gave a wary glance at Boss who was glaring fixedly back at him. "N– n no. I– I mustn't." He stared resolutely at the quickly approaching dock and surf pounding rhythmically on the beach of pure white sand. He drummed his fingers and began to twitch and fidget uncomfortably.

"But Boss said you guys were just going to 'do away with me' anyhow, so what does it matter what stuff you tell me, right?"

Justin looked confused but finally cracked a slight smile, murmuring more to himself than to Zak, "Well, what harm could it possibly do?" Grinning broadly, Zak scooted next to the man who, apparently, was not the sharpest tool in the shed. Testing this guy for info wouldn't be as hard as he had first thought.

"Your job must be really, really hard and important because you look like a smart, strong, diligent, and hard-working man. Am I right?" Zak stated in obvious exaggeration.

"Oh, gosh. All I do is the odd jobs Boss commands me to do. Nothin' special," explained Justin.

"This was going to be entertaining. Keep the words simple, maybe diligent was a little too much for him ... I'd most likely be better off using briefer words from now on," Zak thought, for Justin looked a bit bewildered as he babbled on. The man was obviously quite flattered by the compliments, as shallow and insincere as they were.

"Only problem is, I love to drink. Like to drink all the time," he confessed. And he added, "I get drunk too. 'Fraid Boss'll fire me for it all, but 'e never does. Good man, Jake is.

That's his name, don't 'cha call him that though. He'll blow through the roof he will."

"Jake, Jake … where have I heard that name before?" Zak questioned himself.

"Yep, good guy still." As Justin continued to blabber on, Zak hoped to catch something important and was racking his brain to recall why that name was so familiar. "My family, they live on the island with me too, along with all the others."

Zak interrupted. "Who are 'the others'?"

"Oh, yer not the only one, don't 'cha know. Dozens more like yees." Scratching his chin absently, Justin went on. "Don't like the job too much, but ye know how it is, gotta' keep food on the table and what not. Besides, Boss will never let me leave, not ever. He'd kill me, he would, if ever I tried. Thinks I'd spoil his arrangements and tell his deep, dark secrets. Thinks I'd go blabbing his big, huge plan and the one thing he's been workin' on fer the past six years. Maybe I would," he said, as if contemplating the issue aloud, "then again, maybe I wouldn't … I dunno. Never thought about it much."

Zak was stupefied and starving for more information; he was getting close to something good, he could tell. "What plan is this guy referring to?" Zak wondered. "It must be pretty big and important for him to have spent six years on the project."

"Please, Justin, do go on. Tell me more about this plan."

"Can't," Justin said shortly.

"How come?" asked Zak, disappointed and shocked at the same time.

"'Cause, we're at the dock now," he chuckled. "Talk to ye later. Take care now, you hear?"

"Sure," Zak replied distractedly.

Boss followed by his crony, Croogar, and their captor,

climbed effortfully out of the craft. Zak looked around and murmured, "Yep, this is your typical island all right." Luscious palms created a leafy roof-canopy over a dense jungle infested with tropical creatures. The sun beat down hard on the three, and instantly, Zak began to sweat profusely. Now midmorning, it was balmy and humid, and Zak's apparel clung to his sweaty body like Velcro. He tried to peel his shirt off his stomach, but it returned right back to where it started. Sighing, he wiped the back of his hand across his head.

"C'mon," mumbled Boss. "Let's go." Zak followed obediently. "Lord," he prayed in great desperation, "help me!"

"There must be a pile-up a mile long!" Mr. Fredrickson exclaimed, trying to see through the dense fog that hung over the honking cars, exhaust spewing out of the pipes like water from a waterfall. Mrs. Fredrickson sighed and glanced at her watch.

"Oh dear. If this doesn't clear up soon, we'll miss our flight for sure!" She pressed down the "talk" button on the walkie-talkie Officer Coleman had given her before they left the house. "Officer?"

"Yes, Mrs. Fredrickson? What is it?"

"Isn't there anything you can do about this wretched traffic? We will definitely miss our plane if we're stuck like this much longer." Mr. Fredrickson, hands gripped firmly on the wheel of the car, nodded his agreement with his ex-wife's last statement and grimaced as he examined the car's clock.

"Yes, there is. I'll get to it."

Mrs. Fredrickson grinned broadly as the patrol car's red and blue lights began flashing and the siren began whining. Wee-wea-weeeeee-wea-wee-wea-weeeee … Cars began to make way for the two vehicles, so they could get through.

At the terminal, after the four had passed security and checked their baggage, they chatted in hushed tones while they waited for their plane to arrive.

"So, once we land in San Diego, we're going to the place where we last heard from Zak," Officer Coleman explained. "I don't know if there's much more we can do at that point other than set up another investigation." Seeing the worried and doubtful look on Mrs. Fredrickson's face he quickly added, "And those usually prove to be quite helpful." He gave a reassuring smile.

"Will all passengers who have tickets for Flight 302 to San Diego, California please assemble at the boarding gate? Again, this announcement is for Flight 302," said a cheerful voice on the loud speakers.

"I guess it's time," Officer Gere said. The others nodded and picked up their carry-on items.

"Where are we going?" Zak asked, his patience worn thin.

"I already told you. I can't tell ya that!"

"Oh, fine!" He crossed his arms and stared sullenly out the window. They were now in a rusty jeep driving on a dirt trail through the jungle. A monkey was swinging upside down by its tail, staring blankly at them as they rumbled noisily by. An ape, suspended in midair by a long vine hanging from a colossal tree that stretched up towards the sky, munched happily on a half-ripe banana. Zak was so intrigued by the exotic wildlife and vegetation that he almost didn't realize the vehicle had come to a halt. The jeep was parked in front of a large, rectangular, cement building with a few windows, all barred, at the very top.

As Zak peered at the structure, he thought he glimpsed the form of a small girl with curly pigtails, but when he blinked she vanished. He couldn't be sure if he had really seen her at all. Scratching his head in bewilderment, he wanted to rewind time so he would not have blinked, and he would have been able to see what had happened. But that was out of the question. "Where did the girl go?" he wondered.

"Let's go," muttered Croogar in a fussy tone.

"But where are we going?" queried Zak, curiosity clearly audible in his tone.

"In there," Croogar replied hotly, motioning towards the building in front of them.

"In … there?" Zak asked, slightly worried.

"Yeah. Ya got a problem with it? 'Cause if ya do, you know it don' matter none. You is gonna do what I tell yees to do, ya understand mister?"

"Yeah, I understand fine, Croogar." The three walked briskly up to the front door of the building with Boss leading the way, Croogar bringing up the rear, and Zak sandwiched between them. Boss stuck a key in the lock of the large iron door, and with a turn, it creaked aside with much squeaking, revealing a dark room. Boss flicked on a light switch mounted on the plain concrete wall and some low watt light bulbs flickered hesitantly on, as if they were afraid of the treacherous things their light might illuminate.

"What's this?" Zak asked.

"Home," was the sarcastic reply. A few beds with drab gray

blankets and starched white sheets were lined up in a row in the far right corner of the room. A few night stands stood next to the beds and to the left side of what appeared to be the sleeping quarters, there was a small generator humming quietly. Overall, it didn't look homey or welcoming or the least bit inviting. On the contrary, it looked quite foreboding and creepy, rather frightening actually, not the kind of place one would care to live in. With the way the beds were lined up in rows along the wall, it kind of reminded Zak of Madeline and the twelve little girls, just a lot creepier and more desolate.

"Why am I here?" he asked, staring at everything, which wasn't much.

"You know too much," replied Croogar.

"About what?"

"Well, I ain't gonna tell ya mor'n you already know, 'cause if ya already know it, what's the point in tellin' ya? And if'n ya don't know it, then I would have told ya and then you would certainly know too much."

"Huh?"

"Never mind," Croogar growled, annoyed.

"Croogar, I'm going to go check on them, make sure they don't get themselves into mischief."

"Right-y-o, Boss."

"Keep a keen eye on the boy. Make sure he don't get into trouble either." Croogar saluted and grinned. Boss gave Croogar a look that seemed to convey the question, "What are you waiting for?"

"Oh, right. Kid, we's gonna take ya to yer hotel."

"Who is the 'them' that Boss is going to check on?"

"Jest some other kids, that's all."

"Are they at the hotel, too?"

"Yeah," he snickered, "some of 'em."

"Then where are the others?"

"Dang! You sure ask a lot a questions, you nosey lil' brat. Never you mind all that, boy. Jeese! You sure like to butt into people's business, don't 'cha?" The crotchety old man grabbed Zak and headed for a very small door on the wall beside the beds.

Once outside, the two followed an overgrown path through the jungle to another, nearly identical, cement building. A worn down, weather-beaten sign above the door read "Containment Center." Zak gulped.

"Hey, this isn't a hotel!" he cried in protest. "I'm not going in there. You can't make me!"

"Oh, really?" asked Croogar. Two men appeared out of nowhere, as if on cue, and each grabbed an arm.

"Ow, ouch!" Zak screamed. "Ahhh! That's my arm there; it's injured. Argh! Put me down!" Struggling and kicking didn't work at all, and despite his refusal, pretty soon he found himself inside the building on the cold ground, whimpering pitifully. Croogar left with the men who stationed themselves just outside. The door slammed with a cold resounding groan, which echoed throughout the cavernous building.

Zak remained on the ground, too petrified and full of pain to move. Soon, a number of children ranging in ages from around five to just a bit older than Zak himself began to edge closer and eventually cluster around him.

"What's wrong?" a little girl with large blue eyes wearing a pink jumper asked sympathetically.

"Yeah, why ya cryin'? You don't have to be scared. We were scared too when we first got here, but this place isn't so bad once you get used to it." Zak sniffed as the group of curious kids crowded around him.

"I– I'm not scared," he said stubbornly. "It's just that my arm's injured, and it's really painful."

"Oh," said another girl in a small shy voice. "I'm sorry to hear that."

"What is this place anyway?"

"We're honestly not sure, but every few days some kids are taken away from this containment center by Croogar, and they disappear. We never see them again," explained a boy.

"What's your name?" Zak asked, picking himself off the ground.

"I'm Nicolas. You can call me Nick."

"My name is Zak. Nice to meet you."

"Same." He smiled warmly, really trying to be friendly to the new boy.

"How did you get here, Nick?"

"Well, I'll tell you from the start. Do you believe in God?" he asked rather abruptly. Usually most people wait until they know the other person for a while before throwing out a question as personal as religion.

"Sure I do, I'm a Christian, if that's what you're getting at," Zak replied.

"So are all of us," Nick said, extending his arms to include all the children huddled around the two boys in the center of the room. "And we have all been blessed with certain gifts. For example, my gift is that I have insight, I can tell how people are feeling and sometimes bits of what they are thinking." He gestured to the girl in the pink who had asked Zak what the matter was. "Sara has the gift of empathy. She cares for everyone who feels sad and can almost always make them feel better. Do you see what I mean?" he asked.

Zak nodded slowly, not really seeing what Nick was getting at.

"Well, what is your gift, Zak?"

Zak thought for a bit and then sadly proclaimed, "I don't have one."

"Sure you do! Everyone has a gift," cried Sara. "Even if it's a very small gift, which may seem trivial and insignificant to you, God can use it to do great things!"

"I don't know then. If I do have a gift–,"

"Which you do," Nick interjected.

"The gift I have, well I don't know what it is or how to use it," Zak concluded.

"Oh, sometimes it takes a while to discover what our gifts truly are. But eventually God shines a light upon it, and you are able to use your gift to benefit God's purpose."

"Do continue though, Nick. What do these gifts have to do with anything?"

"You see there is an organization, don't know what they're calling themselves, but they kidnap kids for some big project. They are real secretive, and if someone, anyone, finds out anything they shouldn't have known, … they …" he gulped and with frightened eyes whispered, "get rid of 'em."

"Just like Mr. Coonfeld," Zak muttered. "Maybe that's why they killed him, and when I went to investigate, I found out too much! That's what Croogar was talking about. That's why he refused to tell me anything!"

"What are you saying?" Nick asked, quite lost and confused.

"Oh, I'm not sure if I really have a good lead yet. It's getting there, but I still need more information. There are so many gaps. Tell me, Nick–,"

Zak stopped short when Croogar entered the Containment

Center, clipboard in hand, and face set in a cold expressionless glare.

"Attention! Order! Hey, quit blabberin' and line up!" Everyone scurried to stand stock still in front of his or her beds. Unsure what to do, Zak remained where he was in the center of the room. All the other children, standing tall and straight without making a twitch or movement of the tiniest measure, were utterly quiet.

Seeing the inmates had obeyed his order, Croogar set forth with his intent. "Mary Sheldon, Zak Fredrickson, Nick and Sara Felding, … oh, and Tim Johnson, y'all are comin' with me." The children looked extremely frightened, terror shadowing their faces, glancing at one another as the remaining boys and girls all said silent prayers for them. Zak swallowed hard and led the group out the large iron door.

"Hey, how do they know all our names?" Zak asked, bewildered.

Nick shrugged, "They got connections."

"Well, we'll be safer if we all stick together," Zak whispered to Nick with more confidence than he felt. "The Lord will keep watch over us. 'He tends to his flock like a shepherd: He gathers the lambs in his arms and carries them close to his heart …'—Isaiah 40:11." Nick smiled. The familiar Bible verse was soothing and a great comfort. Sara, worry stricken, pulled on Nick's shirt.

"I'm scared Nick. What will we do? What are they going to do with us?" Nick smiled again, but this time to reassure his frightened sister. "Be strong, Sara. 'This too shall pass.'" He squeezed her tiny hand, which had found its way into his. "We're going to stick together, and we'll be fine."

"That's right," Zak added.

IV. Clues

"What will your beverage be this afternoon, miss?" A pretty, dark-haired flight attendant asked in a sweet voice.

"Oh, I don't want anything right now, thank you." The attendant smiled warmly, nodded and moved her cart down the narrow aisle. "Ed, I cannot stop thinking about Zak ... what if ... what if he's ..."

"Now, now. None of this what-if-ing. I won't take it, Joanne. Do you remember when we used to all go to church together?" Mr. Fredrickson asked timidly.

"Yes, I do. Why do you mention it?"

"Well ... I was thinking, you know, wondering ... if ... why–,"

"Why we ever stopped going?" Mrs. Fredrickson ventured.

"Well, yeah."

"I can't– I can't remember."

"I– I ..." Mr. Fredrickson paused to think. "I ... don't know either." There was a heavy silence. "I guess after you left ... we kind of stopped going." Mrs. Fredrickson looked her ex-husband straight in the eyes.

"Perhaps we should pray. I mean, it couldn't hurt, could it?"

"No. It can't at all. If anything it will help us, don't you think? Let's." The two parents clasped hands, which they had not done in all the bitter years since their divorce, and closed their weary eyes. They poured out their troubles, exposing their greatly troubled hearts to a God that they weren't sure existed. They were taking a leap of faith: a giant leap of faith.

"Okey dokey. Here ya be." The five kids looked out to a huge factory where hundreds of children like them were diligently hammering, nailing, screwing, adjusting, and not talking. Not a cough or a sneeze or a whisper of the tiniest magnitude could be heard amidst the noise. "Get to work!" Croogar snarled viciously.

Nick looked at Zak who took a deep breath and said, "But sir, we don't know how to do it or what it is."

"Do what?" Croogar growled.

Zak stuck his hand toward the assembly line of mute children. "That," he said.

"I don't wanna hear your sob story. I don't have time to show ya exactly what ta do! Jeesh! Figure it out on yer own." He motioned with a lackadaisical wave of his arm toward the children. "They all managed to do it."

"Oh all right," Zak muttered.

"See ya'll kiddies." Croogar smiled a yellow-toothed grin and disappeared, whistling the tune to some unrecognizable song.

Zak walked over to a boy, who looked about the same age as he, and tapped him lightly on the shoulder. "Um … excuse me. We're new here, and we were wondering if you could, you know, show us the ropes. Show us what we're supposed to be doing."

The boy went rigid. Out of the corner of his mouth, the boy uttered the slightest of whispers. It was so incredibly soft one could wonder whether it actually constituted a whisper. "Security cameras hidden everywhere. Just find an open work spot and look like you're busy. You'll get it after a while. It's not that hard."

"Oh ... uh, okay ... thanks, come on guys. We've got to do the best we can. Try to figure it out and get to work." They all fanned out to find a place to do their jobs. Zak picked up a little hammer and found a small screw and matching bolt that he pounded into a nearby metal plate, connecting a pointy-head to a cylindrical shaft.

All that could be heard was the faint tap-tap-tapping of the little instruments and tools along with the quiet whirring of the conveyer belt that snaked all throughout the factory. The completed objects were placed upon the belt that disappeared through an opening big enough for the metal work to slip by, hardly large enough for a child, a very small one, to escape.

"Why am I here? When will I see mom again? Will I live to tell my story? And what are we building? What do these things do? How can I escape? Could I contact my family?" Millions of questions buzzed around in Zak's head like a swarm of pestering gnats or determined misquotes. They were questions he was not sure he wanted to know the answer to. "I don't know what to do ..." Zak fell to his knees and twined his fingers together. "Lord God," he prayed. "Help me out of here. I'm desperate; I'm really lost here." None of the kids turned to stare for fear of some terrible consequence.

Somehow Zak found the strength to hobble over to a worktable and continue to assemble the strange contraptions, whatever they were. Later in the day, all the children were summoned out to the shady courtyard for lunch. Everyone lined up in front of a small fold out table, as they were instructed, and given a cup of lukewarm water, a slice of bread with a piece of moldy cheese on it, and a single carrot stick that was crawling with ants and surrounded by hovering gnats. They were given five minutes to eat and then told harshly to continue working until they were called again for dinner. Once the kids were back inside the warehouse, the conveyer belt, which had come to a sudden halt when they stepped outside, jerked to life.

Zak stole fleeting glances over to Mary, Sarah, Nick, and Tim to see how they were doing. They, like him, appeared to be getting along fine, but deep inside they were terrified for their lives.

"C'mon kiddies. Time for dinner!" Croogar called in an almost singsong voice several hours later. The tone, however, had the sound of slyness. It was the kind of tone a dogcatcher would use when coaxing a stray hound into a net to be taken back to the pound. The children silently assembled in a single file line in front of the table and stepped up to receive a cup of water and a minuscule bowl of under cooked rice.

"Lovely," murmured Zak. "A real banquet, a massive feast, eh?" he quipped, his words dripping with sarcasm.

"You know," one of the girls whispered, "on Sundays we get a piece of fruit ... sometimes."

"Oh, wow!" Zak exclaimed dramatically, placing his hands on his face in mock excitement. "Fruit!" he rolled his eyes.

"You say that now," she continued, rather taken aback by his response to her comment, which was meant to cheer him a bit. "But it's a big deal once you've been here as long as I have." She looked down sadly. "I miss him so much ..." She suddenly began to weep. Zak was not much of a hand at comforting helpless children, which he no longer considered himself to be—no, now he was a man—but he decided to give it a shot.

"Miss who?" he asked gently, trying to sound compassionate and caring.

"My little brother, Andrew. They took him away …" she sniffed and wiped her eyes with the back of her hand as she looked up to meet Zak's sympathetic gaze. "They said he was too much trouble—he got into their stuff. He was only five!"

"It will be all right. You'll see. I am going to get us all out here. Don't worry."

"I'll worry as long as there's a doubt in my mind that there is a way to get off this island!" she retorted in a snappy tone. "They took him away … probably took him underground and buried him alive!" She broke down into tears, wailing and moaning. After a while, after she had composed herself, she sniffled loudly and began again. "What's yer name?" she asked in a timid, meek voice.

"Zak."

"Zak … do you really think we can escape?"

"I don't know," he answered rather uncomfortably. Trying to change the topic, he asked in return, "What's your name?"

"Mary," was the soft response. Zak had remembered her as being one of the kids singled out from the Containment Center.

"I dunno Mary, but I'm gonna sure as heck try."

"Zak?"

"Yeah?"

Before Mary could respond, Croogar blew a shrill whistle and herded the kids to a very overgrown path through the palms and vines and thick vegetation. Though it was mid-September, the air was bitterly cold and the lush green grass, now coated in a silvery blanket of frost, seemed to shiver in the chilly wind.

After a brief hike, the group arrived at a building almost an exact replica of the Containment Center they had left that morning, but this was closer to the factory. They were separated from the other kids who did not work there.

"Here. Now go and sleep, ya lil' devils. I'll come to get yers in the mornin': 5 a.m. sharp! He cackled like an old hag and hobbled off, his slumping figure soon disappeared into the darkness. "I'll be back!" he assured them from the depths of the jungle. His voice echoed through to them with a ghost-like tone to it, and although he was getting ever farther away, it seemed as if his presence was still there among the cowering children, haunting them, never quite leaving them. "I'll be back!"

"Isn't there some way you can get our luggage from New York to here?"

"I vewy sowy ma'am," the Filipino luggage clerk said with a broad smile and thick accent. "Not possible. Vewy faw away fwom here. Take much howers to awwive." The group's luggage had gotten mixed up when their flight was cancelled and they switched planes to get to San Diego. Somehow, their baggage was now all the way in New York!

What was more annoying to them, than the fact that they would have to wait for their belongings to arrive, was the fact that the clerk could not quite pronounce certain letters like "r" and "v," which made him difficult to understand.

"Howewa, we haw vewy nice seat fo you waiting." He gestured to one in a long row of lounge chairs that faced the counter. "You like?"

"No!" snapped Mrs. Fredrickson. "No, I don't like!"

The clerk smiled and shrugged. "I sowwy. Nothing I can do."

Mrs. Fredrickson took a deep breath, trying to compose herself. "Look, I'm searching for my son who was kidnapped, and I don't really care at the moment whether or not I have a comfy seat to sit upon!" she exploded. "All I want right now is my luggage. Is that too much to ask of you, young man?"

He looked at her blankly in the way that foreigners do when they have no clue what you're saying. Then a stupid grin spread across his lips, and he puffed out his chest with pride proclaiming, "Not too much fo me. I can't do it," pronouncing the "it" as if it was the word "eat." "Vewy faw away, not possible." He enunciated each syllable almost in slow motion and with great Philippine diction, as if that would make her understand so that it sounded more like "Ve-wy fa aw-way …"

"Yes, please spare me." The distressed woman massaged her temples, grinding her teeth together. "I think I know the rest. Could you direct me to a pay phone, sir?"

"Certainly, ma'am! Pay phone awound da corner. Very nice pay phone especially fo you. You like?" he said this all as if he was telling her she'd won a million dollars in a free raffle. His facial expressions were almost comical, eyebrows dancing wildly up and down with every word.

To appease him, and mainly because Mrs. Fredrickson wanted to get away, she said, "Yes, yes. Sure, whatever. I like. Come on guys." She motioned for her companions to follow her. "We've got to book a hotel. It is going to be an interesting night with no luggage. Oh well, there is a first time for everything I suppose." Shrugging her carry-on bag higher on up her drooping shoulder, she made her way to the telephone.

Running her bony finger down the list of hotel options on

the large screen beside the phone, Mrs. Fredrickson selected a Holiday Inn and dialed their 1-800 number. "Um, yes. I'd like to book three rooms please."

The clerk on the other end replied, "Certainly ma'am. For how many nights will we have the pleasure of hosting you, may I ask?"

"Oh, just one … I hope."

"All right, now for directions. Where are you located?"

"I am at the airport. Could you send a cab or something?"

"Certainly ma'am. May I have the name of your party?"

"Just Fredrickson will do, thank you."

"Very good. Have a pleasant evening."

"Well?" Mr. Fredrickson asked impatiently as he looked at his ex-wife, leaning comfortably against the wall, arms crossed.

"We'll be staying at the Holiday Inn, and they are kind enough to send a taxi to pick us up right now."

"Well that's splendid!" Officer Gere exclaimed with enthusiasm. "You know, they have impeccable room service there, and the food is marvelous …" her voice trailed off when she realized that their client was rubbing her forehead, struggling to cope with all the stress.

From a perched position on his bed, Zak looked around the dark room, picking out the separate bunks aligned in neat rows along the wall. He saw someone roll over and mumble something in their sleep; they kicked off their sheets and then scrunched into a fetal position in the drafty building. Yawning, Zak decided he should probably try to get some sleep himself. Who knew what the next day had in store for him. Chances were, he would need the rest. Quickly, he surrendered to the fingers of sleep, pulling him ever deeper into the depths of his thoughts, random thoughts, one leading to another, eventually bringing him to the two children …

The kids were older now, probably twelve and fifteen or so, but they were in the same house. The whole ambiance was completely different, however. Instead of lights filtering through windows situated high up in a moderately-sized house, the drapes were drawn. No children's squeals could be heard from outside, instead, it was quiet, deathly silent. Jake stood before his sister, both of them taller and thinner than the previous dream, face drawn in a resolute manner. Silent, like the night surrounding them, tears poured down Amanda's gaunt face, spilling onto her dressing gown.

She uttered a single word. "Why?"

Lips pursed, he threw on an old patched jacket, slung a small pack over his shoulders and replied, "I must … I cannot stay here any longer, Amanda. It grieves me so to leave you, but I have no other option." With a deep breath, he said, "Good bye."

The pain she felt displayed clearly on her face, Amanda watched sadly as her brother walked out the front door and disappeared forever.

As Jake walked briskly down the road, his footsteps echoing in the night, his dear sister's words from earlier that day echoed too, overpowering the sound of his shoes on the pavement.

"But, Jake, where will you go? Will I ever see you again?"

"No, you don't understand. I want to forget this, forget them … forget you," he had added reluctantly. He wanted no ties to his past life; he knew it would be all too painful for him.

"You can't do this to us! To me!" She had pleaded.

"I can, I must, and I will."

Upset, she went off somewhere to think, and he went to plan his escape. Now that he reflected on it, it really wasn't the best way to leave his only sibling behind, but he knew it would be impossible to drag her along. Maybe someday he would go back to rescue her ... someday ... someday.

Zak awoke abruptly from the dream. A connection had been made inside his head, something connecting this place with the characters in his dreams, but he couldn't quite get it. He lay awake for a while, staring at the ceiling high above, lost in thought. Then he had an idea. He was not at all sure that it would help him out of this situation; he was not sure if it was a good idea at all. All he knew was he had an idea, and with nothing better to go on, he decided to try it out.

"Psst! Nick. N-iiii-cK!" Zak cupped his hands around his mouth.

"W-what? Hu? Who is that?" Nick mumbled groggily.

"Nick, it's me, Zak. C'mere."

"Eh, hu?"

"Come over here!" By this time, Zak was losing his patience. Much more of this and they would be worn far too thin. Nick crept cautiously across the warehouse to Zak's cot and knelt beside it, quite frankly annoyed by the disturbance. Perhaps if he had been a bit more awake, it would have shown clearly on his pale face in the shadowy darkness of the warehouse.

"What is it Zak? I'm trying to sleep—or at least I was

trying to sleep, you know."

"I know, I know, but this is important," he replied, acting as if sleep couldn't have been less significant.

"Well, what is it then?"

"I wanted to continue our conversation about gifts. You know everyone's gifts, I am correct about that?"

"Do we have to do this now, man? Look at the time, it's gotta be one o'clock in the morn–," but, with a glance at Zak, who was glaring back at him, he shut his mouth, gathered his thoughts and continued. "Yeah, I know about everybody's. 'Cause kids are coming and going so quickly it is difficult to keep up, but I've got a pretty good idea. But what about gifts?"

"Uhhh, er …" Zak hesitated slightly at the request he was about to ask, "could you tell me the gift that everyone has?"

"EVERYONE'S?!" exclaimed the boy.

"Shhhh!" Zak hissed, clamping his hand firmly over Nick's mouth. In an almost inaudible tone, Zak whispered, "Keep it down! Wouldn't be very pleasant if those macho guys in black came and found us plotting here, would it?"

"P-plotting, what?" Nick asked, confused. "We're not plotting per se, just talking …"

"Hey, ya wanna talk outside?" Zak cut in quickly before his companion could question and speculate exactly what they were doing anymore. Nick shrugged and Zak, who was larger, dragged the boy outside. In the shadow of a colossal palm, Zak plunked down and motioned for his friend to follow suit. "So tell me the gifts," Zak urged. Nick fidgeted and avoided Zak's gaze, looking very much like he would rather have been any other place besides there at that moment. "Come on man! We haven't got all night."

"Fine," Nick submitted to Zak's will and gave in. "But where on Earth do you want me to start, there's just so many!"

"I don't know," Zak replied dismissively. "But you've got to start somewhere, so how about oldest to youngest. The older children will probably be more help anyway, so begin with them."

"Might I ask a question?" Without waiting for a response, Nick pressed on. "Why do you need this information anyway?"

"Don't ask questions now," Zak snapped. "You're wasting time. Now tell me already, darn it!" Practically hollering now, Zak was careful not to let his voice carry through the dense jungle into the ears of Croogar or, worse, Boss.

"Okay, okay. Cool it buddy. Look, first there's Jason. He has the ability to make sense of the seemingly unexplainable. Then there's Delilah who has the gift of patience. Need I say more? Joy has the gift of—you guessed it—happiness! Always perky and excited that girl is," he muttered, almost as if it irked him. "A bit frightening if you ask me. Okay, let me think … who's next?" He paused a moment, deep in thought, fingering a moonstone hung by a strip of leather around his neck. The silence was almost unbearable. If it had not been for the steady rustling of leaves from the frigid night wind, Zak might have gone mad from the lack of noise. "Ah yes, I remember!" He cried with a start, his voice piercing the emptiness of the night like a sword. "There is Eric, how could I ever forget him? He has the gift of the message. He's a dreamer."

"What?" Zak asked, screwing his face up in confusion.

"A dreamer," Nick repeated calmly. "God gives him messages in his dreams and instructs him on what to do. He's a lot like that guy Joseph, in the Bible. He was the one with the Technicolor dreamcoat his father gave him."

"Hmmmm, why can't God tell me what to do? I'm so lost!"

Zak thought. "Oh, I see." Zak mused, nodding. Zak perked his ears and sat perfectly still, trying not to move a muscle. "Hey, I hear something, better get back to bed."

"Yeah, probably should before we get caught," Nick agreed. The boys rushed to the Containment Center and crept back to their cots. Once there, Zak was having difficulty falling back into the peaceful lull of sleep. He thought to himself, there must be some way out of here. "I have to think ..."

And think he did. The boy thought hard, contemplating this, wondering about that, all through the night, and by morning, had formulated a plan. Some kinks needed to be worked out and some wrinkles ironed out, but it was something; it was a start.

"God," Zak prayed desperately, "let this plan work, and if it doesn't, if I fail, please provide me with one that will. I– I really need you right now." He closed his eyes and took a deep, relaxing breath, grinning broadly. In his heart, he knew without an ounce of doubt that God would help him. God always came through, even if it wasn't in Zak's timing, he always answered Zak's prayers, and he knew it would be the same this time.

Bright golden sunlight trickled through the leafy branches surrounding the warehouse where the children were sleeping contentedly. A single fiery red ray of light shone brightly, like a beacon illuminating an object in pitch blackness, across none other than Zak's sleeping cot, warming him and diminishing the cold chill of the uninsulated warehouse left over from the night.

Zak heard a loud crash outside and in seconds Croogar's pockmarked face poked through the doorway. His beady eyes, cold and hollow, surveyed the room. "Get up kiddies. Rise'n shine!" he hollered. "What did ya think, I'd let ya sleep 'till ten? Ha!" He doubled over with laughter, cackling hysterically.

"Come on, hop to it. 'S already six thirty. Actually, we're running way behind schedule. Don't ya remember I told ya five? Well, that was jest to get ya dreading the morning! Ha, ha, ha, ha, ha!" he cackled. "Anyways, we got lots an' lots a work to do, you know." He kept adding in his own personal thoughts on whatever he was talking about as he continued to harass the kids as they rubbed the sleep from their eyes. "Breakfast, what there is of it, will get cold, and will swiftly be devoured by the flies if you don't hurry, ya bunch a lazy, good for nothing bums! Not that I really care what happens to you lot …" The boys and girls scrambled around, tying their shoelaces and attempting to fix their hair that had been tousled in the night, but nobody seemed to have a comb.

"Line up here," Croogar ordered, pointing in front of him. The children assembled in the directed spot and walked silently to receive their meager portion of tasteless and lumpy oatmeal. Afterwards, they were shoved into place in the factory warehouse and told to get to work. The conveyer belt sprang to life and began rolling in a humdrum sort of way, bringing along the pieces the kids were supposed to put together.

Around midday, several new boys and girls arrived and were put to work immediately and, like Zak, left without a word of instruction. To account for the newbies, about half-a-dozen others were taken away to who-knew-where. The new children had looks of pure terror on their pale, gaunt faces and had no clue what to do with the pieces of equipment they were given to assemble. How could they?

The ones who were dragged away were more than a little bit reluctant to leave. At the factory, at least they knew that they were of importance and would not have their lives taken from them. They all—every one of them—kicked and squirmed, struggled and twisted, screamed and wailed, cried and protested to be let free, but were eventually overpowered by the buff men dressed in black.

Zak winced. He knew that if he did not put his plan into action soon he would end up like them with an uncertain and most likely terrible fate.

Croogar came to lead the boys and girls back to the Containment Center that evening, and Zak was relieved. His fingers were sore, stiff, and swollen badly from fitting the little pieces of whatever they were assembling and his legs ached too from standing all day long. Also, his bad arm was throbbing and clearly in need of attendance. Everyone was exhausted and depressed, so Zak flopped down off his flimsy bed knowing perfectly well what he needed to do and walked slowly over to Nick who was chatting with Sarah.

"Look Nick," Zak said as he took a seat at the edge of the bed, "which one's Eric? I need to talk to him right now." The look in Nick's sea green eyes told Zak that this task would not be as easy as he had first thought.

"Zak," Nick whispered with a tone of urgency, "Come closer." He beckoned for Zak to move closer so he could whisper into his ear. "Eric," he gulped, looking as if he did not want to have to tell this news to his friend "was one of the kids who was ..."

"Taken away?" Zak asked, part of him hoping desperately that he was wrong, the other part knowing it was true.

Nick nodded, swallowed and said, "I'm sorry, man." Zak thought for a moment, stumped by this new information. His plan had depended on talking to Eric! "Wait a minute!" he cried. "Where do they take them? W– where do they go?"

"No one knows. All I know is, once you're taken, you never

come back." The boy spoke of the whole idea with terrified reverence, but Zak knew he only feared it because he knew nothing about it, as was so common with human nature.

With a determined gleam in his eyes, Zak whispered, "I'm going to find him."

"What?! You're crazy! You can't go out there alone. Croogar's men will track you down and … destroy you. It's practically committing suicide. Zak, you can't!"

"Do you want to come with me? Then I won't be alone."

Nick's eyes widened, and he gasped, shaking his head vigorously. "No way, man. Never."

"Well, if you won't come with me, then I'll go alone. I have to! For my plan to work, I need Eric. He's critical, absolutely crucial for this to be successful."

"Your plan?"

"I'll tell you about it later, you're important too, so we'll talk sooner or later."

Nick was about to protest, ready with another long string of very logical and convincing reasons why he shouldn't go, but Zak got up and crept outside before he really had a chance. As he carefully shut the door, he whispered, "Goodbye." Nick waved sadly, thinking this would be the last time he ever spoke to him. "Bye," he replied.

"And here are your rooms," the bellhop announced cheerfully. "These are your room keys. Breakfast is from seven until ten thirty. If you need anything, please don't hesitate to contact me or another member of our staff."

"Thank you," Mr. Fredrickson said. "Good night."

"Oh, good night to you, sir." The young man replied as he gratefully accepted Mr. Fredrickson's generous tip for his assistance in showing them to their rooms.

"Well, we should get some rest and go to the airport tomorrow to retrieve our baggage," Officer Coleman suggested. All too tired to utter a verbal response, the others nodded wearily. Mrs. Fredrickson murmured sleepily, "Mr. Fredrickson and I have the room next to both of yours, so we'll see you in the morning."

The next day, following a continental breakfast at the hotel and after picking up their luggage, the foursome stopped in a shady park to plan what to do. "I've got to admit, I'm stumped," Officer Coleman confessed. "Here we are in San Diego, but what can we do?" Everyone pondered that thought, mulling it over in their minds for a while and came up with a few ideas, none of which seemed like they would work.

"Hold on!" Officer Gere cried, "I think I've thought of a possible lead. Why don't we go to the police station and look through the files of stolen cars. Most criminals do not use their own personal vehicles. It's too risky because the local license plates are on file, complete with the date of purchase of each vehicle, information and a photograph of the owner, and other information that could easily be traced to the criminal. But the people who are planning to commit crimes don't want to buy new cars either because, although it takes a little time to process the license plate's information and what not, they still have to register the vehicle at the DMV. So, obviously the only other option is …"

"Car theft!" Officer Coleman cried.

"It's worth a try," Mr. Fredrickson said with noticeable optimism. "Let's go."

The group hailed a bright yellow taxicab and were driven to the police department. With both the police officers for authority, it was not too difficult to gain access to the files they needed. As the two officers and the others skimmed through files documenting the hundreds of stolen cars, trucks, and motorcycles, Officer Gere found something and exclaimed, "Hey everyone! Take a look at this." She took the particular file out of its folder and held it up so everyone could get a good view of the paper. "When we were investigating in Mr. Coonfeld's yard, we found skid marks and were luckily able to get the width and design pattern on the tires."

Then Officer Coleman opened his brief case and rummaged around in some papers. Finally, he extracted a crumpled piece of notebook paper with some notes scribbled hastily on it, which he handed to his partner.

"Here we go," she said happily and with a note of triumph in her voice. "The tires, assuming they are all the same—no mismatched ones—are eleven inches wide and have a distinctive zigzag pattern circling the wheel. Oh, we also found some pieces of gray paint. It could have chipped off of the vehicle, which most likely had been hastily repainted not long before in an attempt to fool or throw off authorities that were searching for the stolen car. If the paint did not come off as a result of a poor paint job, as we are guessing, perhaps it flaked off because the vehicle was simply old, perhaps twenty years or maybe older than that."

Officer Coleman, who had been listening intently, along with Mrs. Fredrickson and Mr. Fredrickson, added, "We also came upon two pairs of skid markings during our investigation. One set was from the back two wheels and was located right near the driveway. It was most likely created when the kidnappers made their getaway. The second pair of skid marks was made from the left back wheel and the left front wheel. Those were probably created when the car made a sharp left turn from Hickory Road onto Walnut Street."

"Wow!" Mr. Fredrickson cried. "How did you find all that? How did you figure that out? Th– that's extraordinary! It's fabulous! It's amazing! You guys are unbelievable!"

With a slight smile on her lips, Officer Gere said bashfully, "It's what we do; it's our job to figure this stuff out."

"Well," Officer Coleman began, "it's a series of logical steps that we utilize. It is a darn good thing that the escape vehicle was old. Otherwise, the brakes wouldn't have locked and produced marks on the pavement. Paint wouldn't have flaked off either, and we would have no leads."

"But what can we do with this information?" queried Mrs. Fredrickson.

"Loads!" Officer Gere exclaimed.

"We can estimate the approximate length of the vehicle because we have one back and one front wheel, and we also have the width because we can figure out the distance between the two back wheels. The dimensions of the escape vehicle are ... hold on a second," he muttered as he scrounged around in his bag. "Aha! Found it. Here we are. The vehicle appears to be a van," he said, studying his notes. "It is four feet by twelve feet."

"This will certainly help things go a little more swiftly," Mr. Fredrickson pointed out.

"And smoothly," Mrs. Fredrickson added. With that additional information, the four continued their search for what they now knew to be a van.

Zak's eyes quickly adjusted to the darkness of the jungle. The only light source was the faint glow of the quarter moon, which filtered through the trees. The boy was not sure exactly where he was going, so he decided to simply follow the path, which had been trampled clear of weeds from heavy trafficking along the route. Now worn down to fine dirt, it crunched softly beneath his feet as he walked through the trees. The soft cry of hunting owls blended with the rustling of tree branches. A variety of foresty sounds, some near, some echoing from a distance, filled the night air. Zak sucked in cool, clean, refreshing air and breathed in deeply. As he carefully picked his way along the path, he arrived at a fork: one branched off to the left and the other wound straight on ahead. He decided to continue going forward and was rewarded when he came across a small cabin. It was illuminated softly by a little lantern set in the front window.

Zak crept through the brush and weeds and peered in the window with the lantern in it. A crouching man had his back to the boy and was stoking a blazing fire in the hearth. Grey smoke billowed out of the chimney and disappeared into the star-speckled sky. It floated lazily upward, fading into the night and dissipated until it was invisible. The man straightened up suddenly and turned around. Zak ducked out of sight just in time, gasping at what a close call that was. Heart speeding up, he regained his courage and collected his thoughts, keeping the plan, and ultimately his goal, in mind to push him onward. Then, after a few minutes, he snuck a glance in through the window and recognized the man's face.

"It's Justin, from the boat!" he cried. Realizing he had shouted the words out loud, Zak put his hand to his mouth, but it was already too late. Justin pivoted and looked straight into Zak's eyes. He frowned, brow creased, and swung open the cabin door. Zak tried to run but his feet got tangled up in the overgrowth. Justin stomped outside and dragged the protesting boy into the cozy cabin.

"What were you doing out there, boy?" Justin asked, dropping Zak onto the hardwood floor. The boy slumped to the ground and made no attempt to escape, run, hide, or respond in any manner. Then, when he saw Justin was not going to do him any harm, he picked himself gingerly off the ground and faced him.

"I– I'm looking for someone," Zak began.

"You're supposed to be at the Containment Center fast asleep in your bed!" growled Justin, agitated.

"Well, yes, I know that but ... I gotta find this one kid."

"I should turn you in, kid. You know the rules. I wonder what the Boss would do with you," he mused, rubbing his chin in thought. "Hmmm ... I wonder ..."

"No! Please don't take me to the Boss!" pleaded Zak, falling to his knees. Being turned in this early in the game would be catastrophic. How would he ever be able to escape if the Boss was watching him day and night?

But Justin's stiff reply startled Zak. "I won't."

"Really?"

"Really. Now I'll pretend this little, er ... confrontation never happened," he paused and glanced outside. "Hey, kid. Get under the bed!" he ordered, scooting the perplexed boy under the twin bed decked out in blue and white sheets. "Wait, what? Why? What's going–," Zak cradled his arm, trying to keep his weight off it to avoid the shooting pains it caused him as he crept under the bed.

"Just do it!" Justin demanded, with a greater sense of urgency in his scratchy voice.

A sharp rapping was heard, and Justin hastened to open the front door. "Boss, Croogar. What a pleasant surprise! What brings you here to my humble abode at this time of night?" He ran his fingers through his gray hair and smiled nervously, trying to conceal his feelings.

"There was an escape from the Containment Center. Someone is running loose out there, and we need to find him. You haven't seen him, have you?"

"Uh, no, n-nobody here sir," he stuttered. "But I'll be sure to keep my eyes peeled."

"Hmm ... yes," Boss said absently. Then he briskly ordered, "Croogar, search the cabin!"

"Yes, sir!" Croogar replied obediently. The old man's beat-up and worn-out sneakers caused the floorboards to creak softly in an almost ominous kind of warning as he practically tore the little home apart.

"Hey, wait a minute," Justin objected, "I already told you. There ain't no one here. You can't–," Boss gave him a menacing look, and Justin immediately swallowed his pride and the comment he had planned to make. Croogar threw open closet doors, tore open dresser drawers and flung the contents all over the room. A sock flew through the air and snagged on the fire poker resting against the hearth, a flannel shirt soared across the room and landed in a heap at the foot of the bed Zak was crouched beneath. All other articles of clothing were soon strewn about the cabin, which, only moments before, had been neat as a pin. Croogar growled and grunted as Boss stood, not attempting to conceal his smirk and obvious contempt, arms folded leaning against the wall, watching.

Then the elderly man began walking slowly over to the bed. Zak held his breath and lay as still as possible, his heart pounding so fast and hard in his rib cage that it hurt.

"Hmmm ..." Croogar uttered, a smug smile slowly creeping across his face. It was freakishly similar to the one Boss was wearing himself as he observed his assistant. Only half a dozen paces away from the bed, Croogar paused and turned to look back at Boss. With a smile of reassurance and a slight hand gesture of permission to continue, Croogar approached Zak's hiding spot. With steps that seemed to last a lifetime for the petrified boy, he eventually arrived at the bed.

Zak thought frantically, and as he felt around on the floor for something—anything—that would help him escape whatever horrible fate Boss and Croogar had in mind for him. He fingered a cold, hard, metal handle and silently gave it a tug. To his delight, a trap door opened up. Grinning widely with relief, Zak scooted over to the door, pulled it open, slid under it, and replaced it soundlessly. All that was under the trapdoor was a small area of scooped out dirt, a little hiding place, almost like a potato cellar. Although cramped, it was better than nothing. There, he sat and listened intently.

Croogar knelt down beside the bed and held up the dust ruffle to peer underneath. His eyes gleamed menacingly. Disappointed that he had failed to capture his helpless prey, the old man threw down the ruffle in disgust, and straightened up.

"Look guys, this is really a waste of time," Justin pointed out. "Where would I hide a child?"

Boss thought for a minute and then muttered, "I– I don't know ..."

With a dissatisfied expression dominating Croogar's already unsightly features, he continued to glare fiercely around the room.

"If you want to take my advice, I'd suggest you search elsewhere on the island. Who knows where a crazed kid could escape to?"

"Yes, come on Croogar. The child is obviously not here. Justin, stay on the lookout."

"Of course, sir," Justin replied. Boss surveyed the cramped cabin suspiciously one last time and saw himself to the door. "Good night," Justin waved and eagerly shut the door behind them. "Whew!" he sighed, wiping his face and neck with a slightly soiled handkerchief.

"That was close." Zak thought, as he crawled cautiously from his hiding space and warily looked around the room. As he brought himself to his feet, he winced with pain from the injured limb.

"Hey," Justin asked with concern, "what happened there?"

"Oh, er, it's nothing, I'm fine. I've got to go."

"No, no, hold yer horses. Le' me take a look a' that."

Reluctantly, Zak proffered his arm to the man, while keeping it bent. Extending it really hurt, so he tried to avoid that.

Justin examined it, running his hand up and down the length of Zak's arm. "Hmm, there's a really bad sprain, but it's not broken. How'd ya do that?"

Zak looked all around the room, shuffling his feet. "Oh, I dunno. Look, I really have to …"

"Here, I can fit you a sling fer that if ya like. It'll hold off the pain fer a bit while it heals." Justin looked kindly into the boy's eyes.

"Sure, why not, if you think it'd help," Zak replied casually. Justin disappeared into what looked to be his bath quarters and returned with a clean white piece of linen cloth. Bending the arm and pressing it to Zak's chest, he wrapped the cloth around the boy's neck and back, tying it securely under his armpit. Then, he carefully adjusted the arm in the sling so it could rest there, undisturbed, and would not be easily jostled.

"There, that should be a little better."

Zak tried it out and found it very difficult to move his arm, which was good. Smiling gratefully he looked up to meet Justin's caring gaze. "Thanks a bunch, Justin, for everything. I owe ya one," he said graciously.

"Ah, it was nothing. Forget it ever happened."

"No really, thanks. This is much better," he indicated his bandaged arm, "and thanks for not squealing on me to Croogar and the Boss, but I'd better get going, people to see, places to go, the whole shebang. Ya know?" Zak strutted toward the door and slunk away into the night, leaving Justin watching forlornly as he walked away.

Zak crept through the tall, dead grass waving in the night breeze that swept the island. The wind seemed to whisper warnings to the young boy as he found the path again. After meandering along for a while, Zak approached a dark hut plated in thin sheet metal. He got closer and looked up and down the shack. Maybe, he thought, that's where they go when they leave the warehouse. It was worth a try. Zak placed his hands on the door handle and pulled. It did not budge. Probably bolted from the inside, thought Zak. He walked around the side of the building, well you could hardly call it a building, a pile of rusted tin would be more suitable. Anyway, he walked around the side of the pile of tin, searching for an alternate way in.

After circling the hut numerous times and finding no such entrance, Zak sat down to think.

He crouched down beside the wall of the shack and looked out into the starry night sky. "You know," he prayed silently, "sometimes I feel you're watching over me from the things you've given us here on Earth. I mean look at that sky! All the constellations are beautiful, spread out on a background of fuzzy velvet. It's like a map of all the spirits of believers around the world, mixed in with a whole bunch of black specks." He picked up a handful of sand, and then muttered, "... though you are as numerous as the grains of sand, I know you each by name and number the hairs on your head." As the last of the cool sand escaped from his fingers, Zak noticed that the structure was built upon sand. "Sand!" he thought. "I can dig in sand!"

He set to work one-handedly clawing frantically at the fine mixture of ground-up rocks and dirt. Within a few minutes of strenuous digging, he had created a hole nearly big enough for him to scuttle under. A little while later, the tunnel was large enough. Still, he could only hope he would find something of use to him inside.

Poking his head in first and using his legs to scoot him through, Zak crawled inside the hole and arrived bruised and slightly scraped, but nevertheless all in one piece, inside the shack. He stood up and brushed himself off as he looked around the room. Much like the Containment Center, there were cheap cots lined up against the walls. Many children, though fewer in number than either of the other places Zak had previously been, were tossing and turning restlessly.

"I wonder," thought Zak, scratching his chin, "which one is Eric?" There really was no way to tell, so Zak began on the left waking every boy.

"Nope, you're Grant?"

"Yeah, what do ya want?"

"Nothin' go back to sleep, sorry for wakin' ya," Zak would say. This went on with Harry, Nelson, Nathan, and finally he came to redheaded boy with about a million freckles scattered about his face.

"Are you Eric?"

"Ah, yeah," Eric replied, rather uncertain as to what significance that was.

"Okay, Eric," Zak said, ready to get right to the point, "Nick Felding and I were talking, and he told me that you are a 'dreamer.'" Eric sat up in his bed and unfolded his glasses, which were stuck in his front shirt pocket, and placed them delicately on his nose.

"Umhhmm," he mused, "yeah, so?"

"I have a plan to break out of here, and I need your help. Will you do it?"

Eric avoided Zak's gaze then rubbed the back of his neck as he mumbled, "I– I don't know."

"What?!" Zak cried in alarm. He had fully expected anyone he asked to help him escape from that dreadful place to, well … do it! Didn't they want to return to their families, their friends, their homes, and their lives? The thought of hesitation—let alone rejection—from any person he asked to assist him in this task had never crossed his mind. "What do you mean, 'I don't know'? Don't you want to help me?" Zak asked.

The boy lifted his head and then slumped back down again. Zak ignored him.

Still not daring to meet Zak's eyes, Eric explained his reasoning. "Well, I mean, it's so sudden. Can't you give me a chance to think it over? Anyway, my faith is a bit …" he paused to choose the best word to use, "it's … a little shaky at the moment. I do not think I trust God enough to help you, at least right now. Come back in a couple months, maybe a year, and I might reconsider. I'm sorry."

Zak raised his eyebrows in furious disbelief. "Next year? Next year?! I don't know if I'll live to see the next day! We haven't got that kind of time, Eric. We need to do something. We need to take action, and we need to do it now!" He grabbed Eric by his bony shoulders and tried to shake some sense into him. "What are you, mad?" Zak shouted, enraged. "This is not about you …" he thought about that for a moment and then added, "or me for that matter. You have to look at the big picture! Think of the hundreds of kids who are suffering on this island and the families who are missing them. We've got to help them!"

"We don't have to help anyone," Eric stated stubbornly, narrowing his eyes at Zak. "And I'm most certainly not helping you. Especially the way you're asking me right now."

Sighing, Zak said, "Look, would you like me to help you iron out the wrinkles in your faith right here, right now so that you could feel confident enough to assist me with this project?"

Looking undecided, a flicker of hope flashed through Eric's eyes. "Hey," he thought, "it couldn't hurt to try." So he shrugged and said, "I guess you could. That is to say, you can try." Then he looked away and sadly began. "See, the thing is, I have so many questions. Like, how do we know that God created the Earth, and it wasn't some freak space explosion or collision or somethin' like all them scientists say?"

"Let's see," Zak said, thinking and formulating his response. "Well, science shows the odds of the creation of our planet occurring as a result of the 'Big Bang theory'—this theory, of course, being that chemicals in space came together, there was a big bang and 'poof' the planets appeared—are so slim that numbers can hardly describe them! Now, the probability of those same chemicals, or others deriving from those original chemicals, aligning so perfectly as to create organisms as complex as human beings is almost like … a zillion to one … or something like that. Our bodies are so amazingly complex, Eric, and without the precise and perfect alignment of our molecular structure, we would not have become the creatures we are today. That means that someone, or something like God, must have created the earth and the creatures that inhabit it. There is no other possible way that our lives could be how they now are. Evolution or pure chance doesn't account for the miracle of life and the millions of miracles that occur everyday!"

At a loss for words, Eric stared dumbfounded at Zak, gapping. After a few moments, letting this explanation and evidence of the existence of God sink in, Eric uttered, "wow!"

"So will you help me?"

Eric nodded vigorously.

"Okay, here's the plan …"

By three o'clock, the quartet still had little luck with their search. But after some wholehearted prayer, they stumbled upon the picture of a van very much like the one they were looking for. "Hey!" Mrs. Fredrickson shrieked, as excited as if she had found the cure for cancer. "Take a look at this," she said, extracting the file from the cabinet.

She handed the folder to Officer Coleman who studied

its contents and then exclaimed, "Mrs. Fredrickson, bless you! This must be the van! Look, here's the picture! Grey in color. It's a 1960s model and right here we have the wheels. They have the zigzagging pattern and here are the dimensions of the vehicle!" He ran his finger down the file and could hardly contain himself, "Four-by-twelve!" He grinned broadly and engaged the equally excited mother in a heartfelt embrace.

"Look here!" Officer Gere pointed out, who had been looking over her partner's shoulder, examining the file, too. "It says that this van was stolen two days before Zak went missing. The man who reported the crime lives only two blocks from here."

"We should go and have a chat with him to see what we can find out," Mr. Fredrickson suggested. Everyone nodded.

"Sounds logical," Officer Coleman concurred.

So, with that, the group left the police station after thanking the manager and walked to 11672 Craneville Lane to speak with the former owner of the van, Orville P. Watkinson.

Craneville Lane was a pleasant street with moderately sized homes on either side. The house at 11672 had a small but neatly trimmed and well-watered lawn, surrounded by fragrant flowers and full, leafy shrubs. Officer Coleman walked along the cement path bordered by colorful stones and magnificent seashells, both of which appeared to have been polished to perfection by the crashing waves of the ocean. The path led right up to the porch steps. The policeman climbed them and rang the doorbell.

"Err ... ah, who is it?" asked a gravely voice from behind the large pine wood door.

"It's the police," replied the Officer primly. The sound of several bolts and locks being undone was heard followed by the door flying open, revealing none other than Orville Watkinson himself. The man appeared to be around sixty years of age and was sporting an old bowling hat, horn-rimmed spectacles, a white button-down shirt, suspenders holding up gray slacks, and brown penny loafers.

"Why, hello. Is there a problem, Officer?" Mr. Watkinson greeted warmly.

"Oh, no, you're not in any trouble, if that's what you mean," Officer Coleman replied, smiling.

"Well, in that case, won't you please come in?"

"Yes, thank you. I'd love to, but may my friends and partner accompany me, Mr. Watkinson?"

"Certainly but … hey, wait. How did you know my name?"

"We'll discuss that later," Officer Coleman said dismissively, hoping that if he did not act as if it was unimportant, then neither would the man. He stepped over the threshold and into the house. Mr. Fredrickson, Mrs. Fredrickson, and Officer Gere followed him inside.

"Make yourselves at home," Mr. Watkinson offered. "Kaaaa-rrrren!" he called out, turning away from the group and cupping both hands around his mouth. "We have guests." He returned his attention to the Officers and their friends and said, "So, what is it you've come to talk to me about?" He queried, as he sat down in an overstuffed armchair positioned so that it was facing Officer Coleman.

"You see," he began, taking a seat on the flower-patterned sofa opposite Mr. Watkinson, "Mrs. Fredrickson's son has been kidnapped, and we believe that the culprits used, and may still be using your vehicle."

"My stolen Volkswagen?" Mr. Watkinson asked, perking up. "That's odd. You're sure it's my vehicle?" he asked, clarifying that there was no sort of mix-up or misunderstanding.

"Quite certain. Yes, um, we were wondering if you could give us some information about your van to help us out."

"Sure," Mr. Watkinson replied willingly.

Mrs. Watkinson entered the room carrying a pot of tea and six cups with a silver tray of tea cakes. "Here you are," she said smiling, as she poured the steaming liquid into the cups and handed them to each person. "Oh! I almost forgot!" she exclaimed, as she scurried back into the kitchen and reappeared a moment later with a bowl of sugar cubes and a pair of silver tongs. "Can't forget the sugar," the plump little lady tittered cheerfully.

"Now, as I was saying," continued Officer Coleman in a matter-of-fact-way, "could you provide us with some info about your car?"

"Yes. Hmm, let me think," he rubbed his forehead, trying to recall his beloved Volkswagen. "Well, I had a locating system installed in my van, but it must have been removed by whoever stole it."

"Do you know where it is now?" asked Officer Gere asked.

"Know where what is? The van you mean? Because if I knew where it was, I think, I would have it parked out front, don't you?"

"Yes, yes, of course, you would. I meant the locating system."

"Good Heavens, no! How would I know a thing like that?"

"Well, do you have the monitor that goes with the locater?" Officer Gere pressed.

"Actually ... I do," he said, as he rummaged through the drawers beside him and pulled it out. "I never thought of that ... hmmm," he mumbled to himself. He handed it to the policewoman and sat back down in his chair.

"This shows exactly where the location of the device is!" Officer Gere cried. "Why didn't you ever try to find it?"

"Actually, I don't know how to work the darn thing," Mr. Watkinson admitted, sheepishly giving a small shy grin.

"It's all right," the officer consoled, "all you have to do is press this button here and … that one there, and then this red one."

"Like this?" Mr. Watkinson asked, pointing to the buttons he should press successively in the proper order.

"Yes, that's exactly right," Officer Gere affirmed.

"I see now." The man nodded his understanding. "S'pose I coulda figured that out on my own …" he added in quiet embarrassment.

"Let's go!" Mr. Fredrickson cried.

"But where to?" his ex-wife asked.

"Why, to find the locator of course!" he replied, as if that was the most obvious response.

"Yes!" they all agreed in unison.

After driving a short distance around town following the directions on the monitor, they arrived at the location indicated and piled out of Mrs. Watkinson's beige '95 Toyota.

"This is the place," Officer Gere confirmed. "Let's have a look around, shall we?"

"What does the locator look like?" Mrs. Fredrickson asked.

"Hmmm … let me think. I haven't seen it for a while. Wait, yes. It's neon green, and it has two black buttons on either side and a larger red one in the center with a small screen similar to the one on the monitor here," Mr. Watkinson replied. With that, Mrs. Watkinson turned off the ignition and milled around with the others as they looked around the courtyard in search of the locater.

Suddenly, a sharp ringing broke the serene silence of

the park. "Oh, um, that must be my walkie-talkie," Officer Coleman murmured to himself as Officer Gere's began to ring as well. They both unclipped the devices from their belts simultaneously and pressed the "talk" button.

"Hello?" Officer Coleman said into his walkie-talkie.

"Er, uhh … Hey– uhh, officers. H– how's it going?"

"Hey, who is this anyway? Headquarters?"

"Yeah, we– uhh, have a new assignment for you. Two other officers will be taking your place. Return to San Francisco immediately. Meet them at terminal twelve at the airport, and they will provide you with your tickets home. You're being reassigned to a homicide case yeah, that's right, homicide." The instructions rushed out in a speedy, nervous flow all together with no pauses, almost as if it was one long sentence.

Officer Coleman was a little confused. Headquarters never talked like that to their officers, and they never reassigned police without first getting their consent, unless something was terribly wrong. Something was a bit strange about this.

"But, but we've been working on this case for a while now, and we might have a lead!"

"No ifs, ands, or buts! Do you understand? Never question the authority of your commanding officer!"

"Y– yes, sir."

"All right then. Over and out!"

"Copy that," he replied dejectedly.

Both police officers had looks of extreme disappointment on their stricken faces. They walked slowly over to the group to explain the situation.

"Here are your bags," Mr. Fredrickson said unhappily, as he unloaded them from Mrs. Watkinson's car. "Best of luck with your new case."

Officers Coleman and Gere could barely manage weak nods. Although they tried to appear hopeful and excited at being assigned to a new case, they struggled to plaster smiles on their faces. They had inevitably become attached to the Fredricksons: Joanne and Ed, and the child they had hoped to find. After all the work they had put into the search for him, now they had to give it all up? It didn't seem right or fair. But they had no choice in the matter, and there was nothing they could do about it.

"Thanks for your help," Mrs. Fredrickson added gratefully. They uttered a feeble, "You're welcome," and hailed a cab to the airport.

V. The Hole

"I need your help to carry out my plan," Zak began.

"How so?" Eric asked.

"Since you are a dreamer, I need you to tell me about some of your dreams and what you think they mean. What is God trying to tell you through them?"

"Uh, okay," replied the boy a little confused, but nevertheless, eager to help. "I'm just warning you, I have lots of dreams, but they don't always make a whole lot of sense, so you're just going to have to make do with whatever you get."

"That's fine. We don't really have any other options," Zak replied curtly, eager to get on with things. Time was not on their side; they had to act quickly.

"I keep having this one dream where there's this island, and I have a bird's eye view, you know, from up above, of all these tall leafy trees and palms, and then we land on the island–," he paused, struggling to remember the precise details. "I think we were in an airplane, or I'm an eagle soaring up above or something. Anyway, somehow, I– I'm in this dark place, and there are many people working." He closed his eyes, trying hard to remember. "It– it is noisy in the dark place, and the men there are barking out orders. I can't quite recall what happens next, but then there's a huge explosion, and everything goes dark and then …" he looked off into space as his voice trailed off to a whisper. "And then, I always wake up."

"What do you think it could possibly mean?" Zak inquired, stumped.

"I've been trying to figure it out for sometime now." He shook his head sullenly, leaning further back on his pillow. "So far, I've got nothing."

The boy next to Eric, who had been moving around earlier, sat up in his bed.

"Hey, I might be able to help," he offered cautiously, unsure of what was going on.

"Um, we don't really need–," Zak began, but then he stopped mid sentence and reconsidered. "Okay. What's your name?"

"Jason."

"Ah! Nick told be a bit about you. You make sense of the seemingly unexplainable, I believe that's what he said."

"That's correct," the dark-haired boy affirmed.

"All right, come over here, and we'll see if we can't use your gift, too," Zak invited, motioning for him to join the two on Eric's already sagging cot.

The boy obeyed and padded over.

"So, what do you think this could mean?" Zak drilled, fixing Jason with a fierce gaze.

Thinking hard, Jason furrowed his brow. The three remained in silence for several long minutes, then the boy looked up, an idea popping into his head.

"You said you have a bird's eye view, right?"

Eric nodded. "Okay, and there's lots of plant life, like an island. Well, I think it's safe to assume that could very well be this island."

"Good, good, keep going," Zak urged.

"Okay, and from what else you described, it sounds to me like it's a factory of sorts, men working in a dark place, perhaps underground ... a big explosion ..." He bit his lip, thinking again. "Maybe," he suggested, eyes wild with the excitement of figuring out a problem, "maybe there's an underground factory, or storage area of some kind on the island. If you keep having this dream, then it's got to be important, God wouldn't be sending it to you repeatedly if it weren't. So, if we locate this place, then maybe it will help us figure out what is going on here and help us escape and go home!"

"Okay, that's good. So now what do we do? How do we find it?"

"If we can get out of here, we can look for it. Because you said you had a bird's eye view," Jason said, looking Eric in the eyes, "that gives me the impression you were in an airplane. Try looking for a cleared area on the island, where there's room for something to be underground without obstructions like deep tree roots and streams messing it up. Also, there may be an airstrip for the probable airplane."

Zak was so excited, he jumped off the bed. "Awesome! I'll get to work right away. This is a great advancement. Thanks so much, both of you. I'm going to get us out of here." Eric was about to reciprocate the gratuities, but instead swallowed his response and stared at the door of the shack, terror clouding his eyes. "Oh, no," he gasped. "Hide!" he ordered, hardly able to get the word out as the door began to rattle violently.

Eric and Jason hopped back into their beds, throwing the covers over their bodies, doing their best to look like they were sleeping. But Zak was caught like a deer in the headlights, unable to move, without a place to hide.

"Come on, come on," a voice was hissing from outside. Then, the door flew open and a blinding light was switched on. Piercing light flooded every corner of the hut, and the sleeping boys and girls groaned slightly and rubbed their eyes at the disturbance. Boss and Croogar appeared, accompanied by four … no, five, they kept filing in one after the other … wait, six other men! Zak gulped as he evaluated the six men dressed in black skintight clothing.

"You!" Boss said, baring his crooked, yellow teeth and pointing a finger at Zak accusingly. The boy felt like an insect under a microscope or an invalid escaping from a mental institution with a great spotlight tracking him. Terrified, he sucked in a quick breath and backed into the corner as the men approached. Quickly gathering his wits about him, Zak drew strength from the spirit he knew was watching over him. Zak did not want to waste time with chitchat so he scurried for the door, dodging both Boss and Croogar along with four of the six men. The last two, the biggest and burliest of the bunch, snagged him and held the boy, dangling him in the air like a rag doll. "Let's go, boys," Boss growled in his accustomed manner, signaling for his men to follow him, as he exited the shack and headed out into the darkness.

Eric looked about ready to fall apart with worry for his new friend, but Zak tried to reassure him that everything would be all right. Shaking his head in contradiction, Eric was implying, "No it won't! Just look at you." Zak smiled and clasped his hands together, closed his eyes, and bowed his head, implying "pray for me." Eric nodded and gave a little wave before his friend disappeared. The door to the hut slammed shut, leaving everyone confused and alone in the darkness.

With an iron grip, the two men grabbed Zak's arms and

carried him roughly through the jungle and out to the dock where he had first arrived at the dreadful, horrid island. Along the way, he was scratched by stray twigs and tree branches and was constantly reminded of the injury to his arm with every step the two men took.

"Ow!" Zak moaned. The men clutched harder still, and the boy winced, grinding his teeth to keep himself from crying out. After some time, Zak saw the reflection of the moon on the smooth surface of the water in the harbor. The foliage thinned out as they approached the water's edge, allowing the twinkling stars to become visible once again in the black sky. They were like precious stones, sprinkled on a length of velvet cloth, enveloping the earth. A small craft was bobbing up and down in the water beneath the sky. Zak was tossed onto the boat roughly and carelessly, as if he was a wooden crate filled with cargo. Then Croogar bound the boy's wrists behind his back with rope. The old man picked up the oars on either side of the boat and began rowing fiercely out to sea.

"What is it with you, kid? Ye jest can't seem to keep outta trouble, eh?" Zak made no attempt to respond but averted his eyes from those of Croogar, which were cold and steely. Croogar pulled on the oars in a steady rhythm. All that could be heard in the dead of the night was the gentle pulsing of the waves on the shore, which was fading slowly away, and the swishing of the water on the paddles, as the rowboat cut quietly through it. Before long, the wrinkled elderly man stuck his oar deep into the water so that it was ploughing slowly now, instead of skimming over the water as before. As he sunk his paddle to stop the rowboat, Croogar jumped onto a much larger vessel anchored to a buoy, which bobbed with the rhythm of the waves. He hoisted Zak onto the boat also and shoved him below deck into a small, cramped room with a tiny window on the sidewall, and a wooden straight-backed chair in the center.

"Don't think of swimmin' back to shore," Croogar growled snidely. "If the piranhas don't eat ya alive, the eels or the crocks will getcha for sure." He cackled evilly then ran up the stairs and out of sight. The boy sighed and hoped with all his heart that his pal back at the shack and his friends at the Containment Center were praying for him at that moment. He took a seat on the chair and was thankful that his captors had been at least courteous enough to provide him with that single, simple comfort. But when he went to sit down, he heard an ear-splitting crack, and one of the legs of the chair broke off. The entire chair gave way. Wood splintered onto the dust-coated floor, and the chair toppled over and sent up a cloud of dust. Zak landed hard on his butt and shielded his eyes, coughing into his sleeve. He slumped slowly to the floor and crawled over to the window. Lying against the wall, Zak listened to the soft sloshing of the water as it thumped against the haul of the boat. With the boat swaying gently to and fro in the night breeze, Zak drifted slowly off to sleep.

He awoke with a start from an absurd dream and felt stiff and sore. Trying to massage his injured arm, Zak realized his hands were still tied together. He wiggled and squirmed and contorted his hands trying to get the ropes loose, but he soon discovered it was of no use. No matter how he moved, the bindings were not going to magically fall off and walk away in search of another pair of wrists. Besides, the more he moved around, the more agitated his arm became, so he gave up. Right then, thumping was heard, and Zak instinctively went silent and still. He could hear deep, strong, masculine voices conversing above on the upper deck, so he sat back to listen.

"How is the assembling going?" one asked.

"Very well sir, we're almost right on schedule."

"Schedule? What schedule?" Zak wondered. A gruff voice, Croogar's most likely, continued.

"So, when do ya think we'll be ready for action?"

"Action?!" Zak gulped, frightened.

"I'm not sure, Croogar. I've counted 175 so far in storage."

"Well, make certain they're well hidden in the hole. We don't want another catastrophe like the one we had to clean up with that one boy ... what was his name, Z something ... Zeek? Zook? Oh, I don't know! It doesn't matter. The point is, we don't want any more mess-ups," a voice that sounded like Boss spat, "–or problems, no more issues."

"Aye aye, captain, sir," Croogar affirmed.

The Boss's voice raised a dozen levels as he hollered, "What have I told you about calling me 'captain'?"

Zak imagined Croogar shrinking back in fear, as a small squeaky voice whispered, "Not to do it ... sir?" he added on as an afterthought.

The Boss shouted back, "Yes!" he sighed, collecting himself and trying to calm down. "Boys, get some shut-eye. We got a big day ahead of us." He emphasized the word "big," which caused Zak to shudder, at the thought of what their idea of a "big day" involved. Zak heard the loud sound of heavy boots, and then it faded to a barely audible tapping as the Boss, Croogar, and the others retired to their individual cabins.

Hmm ... the boy thought. "The hole? Whatever it is, wherever it is, I've got to find it; I've got to go there." That, however, was physically impossible at the moment, so Zak resolved to scheme and focus on freeing himself from the ropes that bound him. Using some large pieces of wood that had gone flying when the chair crashed to pieces, the ropes were sawed off, and then he attended to his raw wrists. "Let me see," he thought, "what could they mean by the 'hole'? And what are 175? 175 of what?" After much thought, Zak could come up with nothing logical and dozed off, having nothing better to do.

Bright, comforting sunlight spilled into Zak's minuscule cabin and woke the boy from his restless sleep. Noise and clatter could be heard on the upper deck: Pots and pans were banging and clanging together noisily above Zak's head in quite an annoying manner. He sat up and yawned, bending his arm a bit and inspecting his chafed wrists. He was about to crawl over to the porthole to have a peek outside when the door to his room creaked open, and Croogar appeared with breakfast. As the old man hobbled painstakingly down the steep stairs, Zak noticed he had two things. In his right hand, he held a plate of French toast drenched in maple syrup, two strips of crisp bacon, two savory sausage links, a fried egg with steam rising off it, a chocolate chip muffin, and a piece of golden-brown buttered toast. That would have been heaven after the moldy bread and bland rice he had been eating for the past several days. Mouth watering, Zak staggered forward, hardly able to believe the magnificent feast before his eyes. But Croogar held it back from him and, grinning a toothy grin, whipped out his left hand, which had been concealed slyly behind his back, revealing the crusty end of an old, stale loaf of bread.

"Na-a-ha," Croogar scolded, "this here's mine! That's fer you. Enjoy!" He motioned to the crust.

Zak tried and failed to hide his disappointment as Croogar placed the bread in front of him and watched sadly, with great longing, as he went back up again.

Nibbling like a sewer rat huddled in a corner, Zak tried to make his food last. Most likely, it would be his only meal of the day, or perhaps for several days, so he had the right idea not simply shoving it all in his mouth, as his stomach was demanding him to do.

The noise level had dropped, and the men were talking again. Listening intently, Zak chewed his bread, hardly tasting it at all.

"Station 2 has reached its quota," one guy announced.

"Ditto for stations 1 and 4," added another.

A different person mumbled, as if he would rather not be heard or noticed but left alone by himself, "We're almost there for station 3."

"Good, good," Boss said. Though Zak was below deck, it sounded as if he was pacing. The boy pictured that grimy, angry man rubbing his filthy hands together while he walked. Then, there was a protesting groan from the deck.

"Oh, how I hate those stupid, idiotic, dumb, mindless Christians," he spat.

"Uhh, Boss?"

"What is it?" he asked, quite bothered by the interruption.

"Er, ah, 'stupid, idiotic,' so on and so on is unnecessary. When you say the first adjective, 'stupid,' are you not also implying that the person is idiotic, dumb, and mindless? Seeing as those are all synonyms for the definition of the first word, that, of course, being 'idiotic'?"

The Boss hesitated at the task of having to sort out the meaning of what the man had just said and growled, "Shut up, Steve!"

"Yes, sir," the voice Zak took to be Steve's replied without a moment's thought or hesitation.

"Those Christians ... they're so ... grrrrr ..." his voice trailed off, lowering to an angry growl and then to a hiss like that of an old-fashioned locomotive or a boiling teapot. "They think they're so great. I'm gonna ... I'm gonna get rid of 'em all!" he boomed at the top of his lungs.

"Yes, Boss," Croogar consoled, "we all know very well how you feel about them. We all agree, too. Don't we boys?" There were numerous grunts of approval and consent.

"All right then. Get to work boys, I want to see some improvement."

"Yes, sir," they all said obediently in unison.

"Oh, no!" Zak thought, horrified. "They're going to, they're going to ki–," he stopped. He could not bear to think it. "I've got to do something," he told himself with great determination. "I must. Now that I've figured out their plan ..." he chuckled to himself. "You're busted!" He smiled with great satisfaction and set to work putting his own plan into action.

"Oh, well. Isn't that a shame?" asked Mr. Watkinson. "They were such nice people."

"Honey, now don't fret. I'm certain they'll send some people who are just as pleasant to be around ... if not more so, than Officers Coleman and Gere."

"I must admit," Mr. Fredrickson added, "those two made a superb team; almost inseparable, they were. And they worked so hard and did so much to help find Zak. I feel bad they couldn't finish the job, you know, so they could know that they helped someone reunite with their lost son. It's no fun doing all the work of hoeing the land, planting the seeds and never getting to see the crops that come to flourish as a result of your own hard work and sweat." Everyone nodded their solemn agreement and set to work.

Mrs. Fredrickson strayed a bit from the group and searched around a shady grove of oaks. "Hey!" she cried, "I think I've found something." She spotted something yellow in color and hurried toward it. "Oh," she muttered in dismay, "it's only a candy wrapper." By that time however, the others were rushing toward her eagerly pressing her with questions.

Mrs. Watkinson asked, "What is it? Did you find the locator?"

"Yes, please tell us, whatever is it?" Mr. Watkinson queried, standing on tiptoe, trying to get a glimpse of the object she had uncovered.

"No, it's nothing," Mrs. Fredrickson replied glumly, holding up the wrapper and displaying how downcast she was feeling. She discarded the trash in the nearest garbage can and continued her search. Just then, a black jeep drove up and stopped by the curb. Two men hopped out dressed in police uniforms with badges on their breast pockets. Mrs. Fredrickson, Mr. Fredrickson, Mr. Watkinson, and Mrs. Watkinson gathered around the two to introduce themselves.

"Hello," Mrs. Fredrickson greeted cordially.

"Good day, madam."

"Oh, Joanne," she insisted, "Please, call me Joanne."

"Of course ma'am," the one replied. "I'm Officer Daniels and this is Officer Benson," Officer Daniels said, gesturing to his partner, who did not smile or look like he wanted to be there at that moment. "We'll be the replacement officers for the ones who were reassigned," he explained solemnly. "We've had a breakthrough with the case, and we'll tell you all about it.

Follow us," Officer Benson ordered.

"My, they got here fast," Mr. Watkinson commented. Everyone agreed.

Setting such a brisk pace that the others had to practically run to keep up, Officer Benson led the group across the street to a large red brick building. "Down here," he instructed, bounding down the steps. Along a dim hallway, around the corner into an even darker room, the group was led.

"Hey, where are we going? Did you guys find a clue down here or what?" Mr. Fredrickson asked suspiciously.

Without replying, Officer Daniels followed them in and flicked on a light. The single low watt bulb, dangling by one wire from the ceiling, illuminated a damp, cold, and foreboding jail cell.

His tone of voice went from pleasant and welcoming to rough and angry as Benson snarled, "In there." He shoved the four into the very same jail cell that Zak had been in. The door was slammed shut, and the men left the room, their footsteps echoing in the long, long hallway, getting fainter and fainter until they were no longer audible at all.

For several minutes, the group was so shocked by the sudden turn of events that they stood motionlessly in the cell, staring at the doorway, as if they were expecting the two to come back and clear up some misunderstanding. After figuring out that was not going to happen, and the whole scenario sunk into their heads—the sheer horror of their reality—some began to panic.

"Oh, no!" Mr. Watkinson wailed, banging his fists against the wrought iron bars of the cell. "We're going to die in here!" Mrs. Fredrickson, however, remained calm. Through her earlier prayers, she felt that God would protect her and everyone else.

"Listen," said Mrs. Fredrickson, in the soothing tone she used when trying to console Zak after a scuffle with bullies at school or after he scraped his knee while learning to ride his bike. "Everything is going to be fine. All you have to do is calm down and take a nice, long, deep breath." She demonstrated, sucking in a great lungful of air. "Breath in ... and out," she exhaled, closing her eyes and relaxing her tense shoulders. But Mr. Watkinson was not listening, he was completely freaking out.

Beginning to hyperventilate from the rapid breathing, he began to whine, "Oh man, oh man! Oh boy, oh boy! Oh God, I think, I think I'm having a panic attack." The look in his eyes said that he thought he wouldn't live to see the next day. He tried to calm down by breathing, "Whooo-eeeee, whoooo-eeeeee," he wheezed, attempting to breathe deeply but merely causing himself to feel more light-headed than before. Mrs. Watkinson walked over to her husband and clamped her hands firmly on his broad and presently shuddering shoulders.

"Orville, get a hold of yourself. Everything is going to turn out all right."

The quartet sat, huddled together for warmth and comfort in the dark cell and waited.

"That's right," Mrs. Fredrickson kept reassuring. "We can be sure that God is watching us at this very moment. There's no need to fear." The group tried to hold firmly to this belief. Still at times, it was hard because it seemed like they had been left for dead. They sat together, remaining silent for the most part; because, what was there to say? There was only so much consoling that could be done by one person. Mostly, they thought. They reflected on their actions and how they had so quickly led to such an inconvenience. Where had they gone wrong? The Fredricksons prayed silently for many things: their rescue, that they would find their son soon, and that everything in this mystery, which was becoming more and more complicated by the minute, would clear up and be sorted out somehow.

The four had no idea how long they were waiting in that cold damp cell. It could have been several hours, or it could have been several days. After a while though—what seemed much, much later—Benson arrived with a key, and the captives allowed themselves to entertain the thought that they were going to be set free, as if nothing had happened. Mr. Watkinson perked up a bit at the thought of it.

However, once they were released from the cell, Daniels, who had turned up shortly after his buddy, handcuffed their hands, blindfolded them, and dragged them down the hall toward the rest rooms. While being carefully monitored, their restraints were removed one-by-one, and they were allowed three minutes each inside the toilets, and then were commanded back out again. After everyone was accommodated, they were escorted roughly back to their cell and locked inside, left alone and afraid, their futures uncertain.

None of the four had any clue what was happening, and so they were extremely frightened. The thing they did not know was that, ironically, getting abducted by those men may have been the best thing that ever happened to them.

Croogar came below deck to fetch Zak. He thumped unevenly down the steep stairs to Zak's place of confinement. He grabbed his elbow, dragging him up on top of the boat into the cool of the early morning and helped him aboard the rowboat that would take them back to shore. When they arrived at the pier, he led Zak to the warehouse to go to work like all the other children.

Once there, Zak chose to work at a spot right beside Eric. When Zak's friend caught a glimpse of him, his face lit up, and he smiled in greeting. Without moving their lips, the two were able to carry on a conversation without any of the Boss's men knowing about it (a skill which most of the kids in the warehouse had mastered by that point).

"Zak!" Eric exclaimed, "Where were you man? I thought you were a goner when I saw them take you away!"

"Thanks for being happy to see me, but that's not important right now," Zak said solemnly. "Right now, I need to explain my plan to you."

"Okay!"

"Look, this is what we've gathered so far–,"

"Wait," Eric cut him off, to his companion's extreme annoyance, "we?"

"Yeah," Zak replied shortly, "your dream and Jason's awesome analysis of it. Now listen!" His command was firm and let Eric know Zak meant business, so he quickly shut his mouth.

"There must be an airstrip somewhere on this island and somewhere near it, in the close vicinity, is a storage place called 'the hole.' When we go outside for lunch, I'm going to sneak away and look for it. Before we are dismissed to go back to the Containment Center, I'll be back. I will tell you where it is, and at eleven o'clock, you will meet me there, all right?"

Eric reiterated the scheme to Zak to make sure he had everything right and asked, "So we'll rendezvous at the

Containment Center, then go to 'the hole' at eleven tonight?"

"You got it!" Zak affirmed with a grin.

"All right, man, I got your back."

"Thanks," Zak replied with a smile. It was nice to know he had at least one advocate.

When the lunch bell rang, Zak gave a fleeting glance to Eric, and no one noticed when he disappeared into the undergrowth. Zak parted the branches of the trees that obscured his path and hiked through the jungle. Eventually, he came to a flat cleared area with no trees or bushes at all.

"Hmmm ..." Zak muttered, inspecting the area. It was very, very large, about the size of a football field, and covered in grass. Eyeing the area suspiciously, Zak walked a ways and discovered a paved portion of ground, cleared of leaves, sticks, and debris. About three hundred yards long, it stretched parallel to the field like a wide sidewalk.

"This is the airstrip from Eric's dream!" shouted Zak with enthusiasm. "Yes, I've found it! Now, where could 'the hole' be?" He scanned the field, standing at a distance, hidden in the foliage. The last thing Zak wanted was to be seen. He couldn't begin to imagine what Boss's men would do to him if they found him there, snooping around.

Cautiously, after checking the sky for planes and surveying the surrounding area for unwanted visitors, Zak inched closer to the cleared area. First putting his one foot out and testing his weight on the ground and then the other, Zak got about three feet in from the jungle when he felt the ground give way. Jumping back with surprise and uttering a soft cry, Zak watched as the whole field began to fall away into a big black hole. Piece-by-piece, it crumbled away until all that remained was a great, huge, gaping abyss.

"Score!" Zak said to himself. "I've found the air strip and 'the hole'! And this is your daily double!" he joked, quoting from *Jeopardy*. Punching the air, Zak prided himself on his good locating skills. Without going down to look in the hole, Zak ran back to the warehouse with excitement to tell Eric.

Panting and slightly out of breath, Zak arrived at the designated meeting spot. "Eric, Eric!" he shouted. Eric looked over his shoulder as Zak sidled inside and called to his friend in a staged whisper. "I've found it," he mouthed, walking up to his work place.

"Really?" Eric asked in astonished disbelief.

Zak nodded and then gave directions as how to get there. "Remember," he told Eric, "eleven o'clock."

"Yep," Eric replied, "I'll be there." Zak smiled and felt reassured. Maybe his plan would work out after all.

Later that night, when the other boys and girls were asleep, Zak crept away from the boat after rowing stealthily ashore. Eric also stole away at the predetermined time. As they carefully picked their way through the dark jungle, both were very wary of every sound they heard and every shape that seemed out of the ordinary, but mostly, of Croogar and his assistants. As they approached the hole, Zak caught sight of his companion and ran to meet him.

"Great," Zak complimented, "you found it."

"Yeah, I did," Eric replied then muttered something under his breath.

"What did you say?" Zak asked.

"Oh, nothing. It's just, this place reminds me a lot of that one dream I'm always having, you know, the one I told you about ..."

They got closer, and Eric said, "Yes, this is exactly the

place! So, hey, where is the 'hole'?"

Zak grinned and pointed to the grassy area.

"That's the hole?" Eric asked skeptically, "but it's only a field."

He looked confused so, without saying anything, Zak stepped forward and watched for the second time that day, only this time with Eric, as the ground crumbled away as before.

Eric's eyes grew as big as frying pans and his jaw dropped to his chest.

"Wow!" he cried. "That was amazing!"

"Yeah, I know, but come on," he said, "we've got a lot of work to do." Zak circled the perimeter of the hole. "I wonder how you get down there ..." he mumbled.

"Maybe there's like a secret elevator or something!" Zak's companion suggested hopefully.

"Mmmm, doubt it. That would be too ... I dunno, too much hassle for a temporary facility such as this. I really don't think it's an elevator though."

The two continued to shuffle slowly around the hole in search of a means to enter its black fathomable depths. "What about ... a staircase?" Eric asked.

"Very possible ..."

"Well then, here you are, sir!" Eric proclaimed, pointing to a staircase hidden in a shadowy corner.

"Excellent! Good work!" Zak commended as he approached the place his pal was indicating. It was very, very dark. So dark, in fact, that the boys could not see their hands in front of them. "You got a light?" Zak asked.

"Naa," Eric replied, emptying his pants pockets with a frown.

"Darn. Guess we'll have to brave it without one." They

inched their way carefully down the steep, steep stairs and finally arrived at ground level.

"I can't see a thing!" complained Eric as he bumped into a wall. "Phaewaa!" he cried, spitting out a mouthful of dirt. "Bleagh! The walls are," he paused wiping his tongue on his sleeve and spitting out more dirt, "pphh, elgh, made of dirt, yuck!"

"Well, yeah!" Zak said, as if it was the most obvious thing in the world. "You don't think they're gonna install nice plastered ones, do ya? Why would they spend the time, money, and energy in that? The place we sleep is little more than a garden shed for crying out loud!"

"Yeah, guess your right. It—yuck, plech—it tastes bad."

To avoid finding himself in the same uncomfortable predicament as his friend, Zak stuck his right arm straight out in front of him like a blind man, as his left was still pinned to his chest, and felt his way along the wall with his mate following suit.

"Wait!" Zak exclaimed suddenly. He dug his hand deep into the back pocket of his jeans producing his state of the art, oakwood Swiss army knife that his father had given him for joining cub scouts. Although Zak had quit after a few months, he still carried it with him everywhere he went for emergencies. Inside the tiny compact device there was, of course, a small whittling knife, a tiny pair of toe nail clippers (in case you get a really painful hang nail he supposed), a minute pair of scissors (although he couldn't for the life of him figure out what on Earth they would be able to cut that he was not strong enough to break on his own), tweezers, and most importantly, a flashlight!

"Come on, man," Eric said. "This is no time for whittling

wooden figurines. We've got a job to do. You said it yourself."

"No," Zak scolded his friend's ignorance, "there's a flashlight in here. I'm not stupid. You know I wouldn't waste time doing such an idle activity at a time like this."

"Oh," Eric replied meekly. "'Course not."

Turning the thing on was of little use, but it was a heck of a lot better than what they had before, which was nothing. The small beam of light led the boys down the narrow underground tunnel. Eventually, after walking for some time, they arrived at a large, open room lit with candles stuck into the walls. In the center of the room was a small circular container. The boys eagerly walked toward it, the contents a complete and mystifying enigma to them both.

"What would they try to hide in here?" Eric asked skeptically.

Zak shrugged in response, equally stumped. Looking over the box, Zak noticed it had hinges on one end, so he lifted the cover and peered inside.

"What is in there?" queried Eric, going closer to see for himself.

"I dunno," Zak replied. He stuck his hand inside and pulled out the contents of the container: a single piece of computer paper. There were a whole lot of extremely complicated-looking formulas, and at the very bottom, an illegible signature.

Eric was getting impatient waiting for his friend to read the paper so he snapped, "Let's go man. It's probably not important. There is obviously nothing down here. Maybe the Boss was purposely leading you here so that he could trap you or something."

"Do you really think so?" Zak asked replacing the paper in the box and giving the comment some thought.

"I don't know," Eric muttered dismissively. It was becoming clear that he was getting frightened, and the longer they spent down in the hole, the more his feeling of uncertainty rose. "But let's get outta here before they catch us. For all we know, we could have tripped an invisible sensor that triggered an alarm, and now, all those macho guys in black could be headed right for us!" He gulped, eyes swinging paranoid around the room. In a forced whisper he added, "We could be right in the middle of a complicated booby trap!"

"Maybe," Zak muttered, not convinced. At that moment, the flashlight went completely dead and a huge gust of wind rattled through the cavern, blowing out the candles. The whole room darkened and went black.

"Lovely," Zak groaned.

"Okay, now what are we going to do?" Eric asked, annoyed, worry edging his voice.

"Look, will you calm down?" Zak asked, rather irritated.

Eric grumbled and said, "I guess we'll have to feel our way back. There's nothing here for us that will be useful anyway."

The two felt their way back along the earthen wall. Zak placed his right hand on the side of the tunnel and began to slide it along. Reaching for the wall, he touched one of the unlit candles. With a whoosh of ignition, it magically relit itself as if an invisible person had struck a match and set the wick aglow.

"Wow! Did you see that?" gasped Eric.

Zak looked at his friend. "Did I see that? Did I see that?! I was right in front of it! I– I made it happen!"

"That was so cool!"

Then as suddenly, flames leapt up into the rest of the candles and brought them to life again, as music brings dancers to their feet when a tune is struck up. The flames danced and threw shadows against the walls as if they were being tossed about from an unseen wind or draft. Eric shook his head in disbelief as Zak watched, open-mouthed. Mouth still gaping like a codfish, Zak stepped forward and gingerly stroked the candle to test that it had actually happened. That it was real.

"It's like ... magic," he whispered, speaking as if he allowed his voice to rise too much, if he spoke too loudly, it would all disappear and it turn out to be a trick in his mind. Eric also wanted to get a better look and put his left foot forward to make his way closer, but he stumbled on a stone and grabbed Zak for support, who, as a result of the sudden shift of weight placed upon him, fell, arms flailing wildly. His hand hit the candlestick, and it lowered mechanically, slowly but steadily, in a manner that suggested there were many mechanisms hidden behind the wall causing it to move. From the ground, the two boys stared, limbs still entwined together from the fall. "L– look!" Zak shouted, frightened by what he had seen.

But Eric was not looking at the candle. He was gazing at the center of the room where the box had been. The floor of the ground was lowering down to reveal another room. Without staring much longer, Zak and Eric untangled themselves and jumped up to look below. Unseen light fixtures illuminated a deep, cavernous room and leading to the room on two sides were long, narrow passageways.

"Let's go!" Zak cried eagerly.

Eric, however, was hesitant. "I don't know about this."

Zak scowled and took hold of his companion's arm, pulling him along, down the stairs and into the room.

"It's the hole!" Zak exclaimed. "It's got to be!"

"What? What are you talking about? I thought that was the hole ..." Eric asked, not quite following.

"You know. The hole. It's the storage place for whatever it is they are hiding, whatever they are having us manufacture on this island: this is it!"

"But, this is just a room. There's nothing hidden in here," he pointed out.

"Well," Zak said, thinking. "Maybe it is down one of these passageways here," he wondered aloud. Dragging Eric behind him, Zak chose the passage to the left and set off. They walked for about two minutes and came upon a fork. Their choices were either go to the left or straight on ahead. Without pausing to contemplate, Zak chose the passage straight ahead. Soon, they could hear faint noises, and a patch of light was visible at the end of the tunnel.

"Shhhhh!" hissed Zak, as Eric began to comment on what could possibly be awaiting them at the far end. He flattened himself against the wall and perked up his ears to listen. Eric, observing his friend, did the same. Deep voices were conversing in angry tones, and one was shouting quite loudly.

"That boy's escaped! How could you have let him escape?" he demanded. "How could you let him escape, again?!" he asked once more for emphasis.

Defensively, another said, "I didn't let him escape, it wasn't my responsibility to keep watch over the little devil. It was Justin's job, sir, not mine."

Someone grumbled something, and then his voice rose to a shout. "You worthless assistant!" The man threw down something heavy, which thudded down on the ground. Zak heard the man's footsteps, so he grabbed onto Eric's T-shirt and pulled him into a side passageway. They crouched down and waited silently in the shadows.

The Boss appeared, angrier than Zak had ever seen him,

with a flashlight in his hand. He swung the beam around the main tunnel but made a right turn into the passage leading off of it, the one the boys were hiding in. Eric gasped in fright but Zak quickly clamped a sweaty hand over his friend's mouth. Boss's large frame blocked nearly all of the light coming into the tunnel. He appeared to the boys as a dark outline panting with fury and hunched over slightly. The sight was quite terrifying and unpleasant to behold. The Boss turned around jerkily and swung his flashlight around with him. Zak gulped and tried not to breath. Narrowing his eyes suspiciously, Boss walked closer to the boys. Eric was panicking, but he, too, tried desperately to remain still and silent. "Maybe, just maybe, the shadows will conceal us enough that he won't be able to see us," Zak hoped.

"I know you're here," Boss whispered haughtily, "and I am going to find you," he sneered. Then, as if he had known exactly where Zak and Eric had been the entire time, he aimed the beam of light right at them. The glow reflected in their terror-filled eyes as they gazed up at him in horror at their being discovered. "Aha!" he exclaimed, as he crept to close in on them. But they were up and running down the tunnel before he could lay a finger on either of them. Hearts pounding, the two sped along with the Boss in hot pursuit. Eric had a look of pure terror in his eyes, but Zak displayed determination in his. It was clearly visible all across his face. They ran as fast as their legs would carry them, praying that they would not run smack-dab into a wall in the faint light they had to guide them. Basically, all they had was God to guide them out safely.

Ever so often, Zak would turn his head to see if they were still being followed, and every time he would see the Boss's despicable face, half in shadow, staring back at him with loathsome, beady, black eyes. Eric stumbled on a rock in their path, and Zak heard him fall. He hurried back to help, but the boy had injured himself. Zak could see that their follower was getting closer and closer by the second.

"Come on!" Zak urged, trying to hurry his friend along.

"I can't," Eric protested, gazing up at Zak in defeat. "J– just go ... leave me."

"No way!" Zak knelt down to assist him, but by that time, the Boss had caught up. A large man, he was quite out of breath from the chase but filled to the brim with rage. Zak managed to get Eric up with his good arm, and he began hobbling along with the boy limping beside him as best he could. The Boss was panting heavily and wiped the back of his hand quickly across his brow, growling a deep, guttural growl of obvious dissatisfaction.

"Get back here!" he ordered, so livid that his voice cracked and squeaked like a poorly oiled hinge. He sprinted forward lunging at Eric, and thankfully, he missed. However, boiling over with fury, he picked himself up and with a loud, "Aarrggggh!" leapt for Zak's chum once more and crushed him flat to the ground. "One down, one to go!" he growled, abandoning the motionless body and glaring at Zak. Soon enough, the man was lumbering forward again. For lack of a more promising idea, Zak kept on running.

He reached a dead-end. "Oh, no!" he groaned. A large pile of boulders barricaded his path, but at the very top, a starry sky was visible. "A way out!" He thought triumphantly. Just as Boss approached the pile of rocks, Zak began scrambling up, with considerable difficulty given the condition of his arm, sending a shower of dust and pebbles down on the Boss and stroking his anger.

With a smile of pleasure and victory, Zak climbed swiftly

through the narrow opening, not much bigger than he was. His arm remained tucked into his chest with the help of the sling. The boy slunk around toward the trees and bushes where he could hide. He had not taken but two steps when he heard crunching noises like the sound of snapping, dead leaves and twigs being stepped on and low voices whispering to one another. Zak did not wait a moment. Scanning the area quickly, he ran lightly across the grass, spotting a way to remain unseen. Skillfully, he shimmied up a tree, curling both legs around the narrow trunk and using his good arm to grab onto limbs and vines and things to hoist him upward into the higher branches. Once up high enough, there he lay, clutching the bark for support, listening and plotting.

"… yeah, Boss wanted us to check on the missiles. Oops! Did I say missiles? I meant the project in the hole," one shadowy figure said.

Another figure, slightly shorter than the other, muttered, "I think the real reason he sent us down here is to look for the boy. He said he got loose again."

"Again?!" the first man asked in disbelief.

"Yep."

"Man, he's like a snake, quick and sly as can be and full of poisonous venom. He's got a ton of tricks up his sleeve. Must know every trick in the book!" The short man nodded and looked over the field.

"Well, guess we can go back now, doesn't look like he's here. Wanna play some poker? Beer's on me!" But the other man was not listening. He was looking straight up at Zak. The boy had gotten so involved in the men's conversation that he had loosened his grip on the tree and slipped. His body scraping against the rough bark created a grating sound, which the tall man had detected. Zak dangled by one arm, luckily the uninjured one, thirty feet above the ground. As he rocked gently to and fro, Zak could feel his hand weakening, and he gulped in fear. "Please, oh Lord," he prayed as he had so often, "keep me safe. I have a plan that will glorify your name. I want to live to fulfill my duty as your loyal child."

"Look, look up there Steve," the tall man said, jabbing his companion in the ribs and pointing.

"Jerry, I don't see nothin'," Steve grumbled, squinting his eyes and looking up in the direction that his cohort was indicating. Steve swiveled around and stood petrified. He was stuttering and tapping Jerry on the arm. "Uh, uh, uh–,"

"What? What is it?" Jerry asked, annoyed. When he saw the razor-sharp teeth and curved ivory claws glinting in the white light of the moon, he grabbed hold of his partner and dashed off, crashing through the underbrush in a flash. The magnificent tiger extended it's front paws out, retracting his very own set of lethal knives in a hypnotic motion. It stretched, almost as if in a bow, low to the ground, his claws scraping the dirt before it yawned, and then sauntered off into the darkness without so much as a suggestion of a growl.

VI. Action

The four had unwillingly drifted off to sleep. They wanted to stand guard in case Officer Coleman and Gere's imposter replacements returned. But after several hours, they could no longer resist the call of weariness. Mr. Fredrickson was sitting, back against the cold, cement wall with Mrs. Fredrickson resting her head on his shoulder. Mr. and Mrs. Watkinson were snuggled up together in a dark corner, both snoring loudly. They had been dozing for quite some time when Daniels strode in and banged his key ring along the bars until he arrived at the door. Flipping through the numerous keys of all shapes, colors, and sizes, he found the correct one and stuck it in the hole.

Mr. Fredrickson and his ex-wife twitched but did not awaken. As Daniels turned the shiny brass key in the lock and flung open the door, it emitted a horrible piercing squeaking sound that echoed off the walls and reverberated throughout the room. The sleeping adults awoke with a start and rubbed their eyes, trying to get their bearings.

"W– who are you?" Mr. Watkinson demanded.

"I thought we already went through this," Daniels said in exasperation.

"Well, you said you've come to take Officer Coleman and Gere's spots, but not why. Besides, we don't buy that for a minute. We know you're not real policemen. Otherwise, you would be helping us find their son, not locking us up for no reason in cells!"

Just then Benson sauntered in, whistling as if it were just a normal day for him.

"Oh dear, they've caught on," Daniels said to his partner, acting surprised. "Whatever will we do now?" His voice was slow and deliberate, as if reciting lines from a play very poorly. Benson shook his head and chortled. "Look, so you've caught on. Oh well, we expected that, sooner or later. Well, I suppose we might as well tell you now, that you know our little ... secret."

"Please," Mr. Fredrickson encouraged.

The two giggled girlishly to each other. "Okay." Dan took a breath. "You were right, we aren't really cops. We work for a very important man who, well, let's just say, he's not on the good side with the law. And, he's done some things maybe most people would frown upon. He sent us here to keep you out of the way of his big plans. Wouldn't want you to spoil it, now would we?" He stole a glance at his partner, smirking in the corner. "So, we prank called the officers working with you, saying they had been reassigned. Then we pretended to be their fill-ins. There, ya happy?"

Jumping up protectively, Mr. Fredrickson stated, "No, we're not. Tell me where my boy is!"

The man smiled a sly toothy grin and looked Mr. Fredrickson in the eyes with such fierceness that he was frightened deep within. The smile soon was transformed into a despicable frown and a look of great displeasure. Then, Daniels said innocently, "Funny, I was coming down here to take you to where you're son is, but ..." he smiled a horrible, greedy smile, hiding many things beneath its false surface, "I don't know for sure anymore. After this outrage, do you really deserve such a treat?"

Daniels touched his index finger to his pursed lips, as if to seriously consider the question. When Daniels and Benson turned back around again, they both bore identical smiles of cleverness and wickedness.

"Okay," Benson said hotly, hardly containing his pleasure, "you can go."

"What's the catch?" Mr. Watkinson asked suspiciously. "There's always something, a reason, a hidden motive. Why else would you suddenly display this random act of kindness? There's got to be a trick in this somewhere."

"Oh, no catch," Benson reassured, still grinning horribly. "Come with us."

Very warily, Mrs. Fredrickson, Mr. Fredrickson, and Mr. and Mrs. Watkinson exited the jail cell and followed their captors.

"We're jest gonna have to blindfold ya again," Daniels said, wrapping cloths around their frightened eyes. They were led down the very same hallway, up the very same stairs, and shoved into the very same van that Zak had been, although none of them knew it at the time.

A rough and bumpy ride in the van resulted in them being jolted and banged violently against the sides. Soon they arrived at the harbor, miraculously, each of them all in one piece. It was about seven o'clock, and the sun was setting in the west, the last rays of sunlight glinted off the shimmering water. It would be dark soon, and nobody would wonder where the four were.

No one would come searching for the missing people because nobody knew they were gone.

Zak fell softly to the ground and sank to his knees in supplication toward God.

"Thank you!" he cried, tears of joy streaming down his cheeks. Clasping his outstretched hands together, he whispered, "You work in amazing ways, Lord. Thank you for sparing my life. Trust me, you'll be thankful for that. I will not waste the opportunity you have given me."

He arose from the sodden earth, looking around. Immediately, he knew where his friend was. Not knowing how he had gained that knowledge, he set out along the path back toward the Containment Center. The moon shone brightly, illuminating hazardous obstacles as Zak ran through the jungle. He made a turn here and backtracked there, taking note of noticeable landmarks he could use to find his way back to the hole quickly.

Zak reached the place where he knew in his heart his friend was and tiptoed closer. He slunk nearer to the entrance with a broad smile upon his face, as weary as he was. As he turned the corner of the makeshift building, he caught his breath. He saw two guards standing at the door, blocking escapees from going out and rescuers like Zak from going inside.

"Shoot!" Zak muttered angrily under his breath. The guards were hefty, broad-shouldered, with heavy-duty machine guns slung over their backs. They were extremely fierce-looking with short-cropped black hair and muscles bulging out in every direction. Neither was blinking. Both were surveying the surrounding area, ready to pounce at the first signs of movement.

Zak crept around the backside of the Containment Center to where he remembered seeing a window. He poked his head up to peer through. Eric was lying on the cold floor, and he appeared to have several bandages wrapped loosely around his injured limbs. Scooping up a handful of pebbles, Zak began throwing them at the window. Eric heard the noise and painfully made his way over. The sorrowful expression shadowing his face lifted once he saw his loyal buddy.

"You came back for me!" he exclaimed in excitement.

"Of course," replied Zak, "I could never abandon you." He beckoned for Eric to come closer. With Zak pushing from the outside and Eric pulling from within, they managed to open the window enough for Eric to climb out. He landed with a thud on the grass, coated with crystal beads of dew, and scampered after Zak who was already headed toward a barely visible path in the waning moonlight.

"Quick!" Zak ordered, glaring back at his friend who was struggling to catch up.

"It will be morning soon, and we can't wait that long."

"Why not?" Eric queried, reaching Zak's side and giving a questioning look. Zak shook his head and waved his arm, dismissing the question. Along the path, they reached the same familiar fork and without a moment's hesitation, continued going straight.

"Where are we going?"

"You'll see ..." Zak replied. Holding a branch aside, Zak motioned for Eric to go on toward the cabin aglow with warm lantern light, which spilled out from the bare windows. In one of them, was an intent face looking out into the field.

"There!" pointed Zak, ushering his friend on. The front door was slightly ajar, so Zak pushed it all the way open and stormed inside, eyes shining with excitement and anticipation.

"Justin! Justin, my man!" Zak cried, jumping up and down.

"I've been expectin' you," Justin stated casually, taking a long swig from a half empty bottle of wine. He staggered toward Zak who took a step backward.

"When I heard there was trouble at the hole, I was suspectin' it was you. What's a matter boy?" he asked, noticing Zak's perturbed facial expression.

"You– you're drunk," Zak spat disgustedly. He made a face at the unshaven man and took a look around the room. It was in disarray: clothes strewn on the backs of chairs and on the dusty floor, broken beer bottles littered the floor area around the garbage can, and bits of chips sat in little heaps around the kitchen table.

"Where's the family you were telling me about back when we first met on the boat? Don't you care that they see you like this?"

Justin looked down at the floor, managing to feel shameful even in such an intoxicated state. "Well, I d'in tell ya the whole truth. See, I had a wife an some kids, but they left me 'for I came to work fer Jake. I jest like to tell mysel' that they's still around ... makes me feel better."

"But, come on man, how long have you been like this?" Zak asked, returning his gaze to Justin. The man gave a foolish smile and attempted to look at his watch. Screwing up his eyes, he put his face really close to his wrist.

"Hmmm, dunno. Maybe three, two, three, five hours?" he replied, looking a bit confused and saying the statement almost as if he was asking Zak.

Not sure what else to do or say Justin asked, "Want some?" proffering the bottle to Zak.

"Um, no thanks, I think I'll pass," he said, with a little smile. Wine sloshed on the floor and splattered, mixing with the fallen potato chip crumbs. "Look Justin," Zak cut to the chase, "who keeps the master key?"

Justin pursed his lips together and tapped his chin thoughtfully.

"Wutdya mean?" Pronouncing the "what do you" as if it were all one word strewn together.

Zak sighed in irritation. "You know, the big key that unlocks everything on the island, the Containment Center, the working facilities, all that."

"Oh!" Justin scratched his chin, thinking. "I suppose that would be the guards," he concluded in a slurred voice, looking up.

"All of 'em?"

"Yup. I s'pose they all got a set," Justin thought aloud, scratching his stubble again.

"Great!" Zak shouted, hooking his arm around Eric, who had been standing motionless and mute, and pulling the bewildered boy along with him.

"You two drive safe now!" Justin called after them with a sloppy wave.

Running into the jungle, Zak explained his plan to his friend.

"Sounds good."

They reached the hole, and Zak stepped onto the open field, and the ground fell away, as it had before: down the stairs and along the tunnel. The beam from Zak's flashlight, which seemed to recharge on its own, led the way. When they got within view of the big room at the end of the corridor, he stood still with horror.

"Guards!" Eric whispered. "What are we gonna do?"

"Hold it a minute, I think I know the thing." Suddenly, Zak shouted at the top of his lungs, "Look, fire! Quickly, get out of here before it's too late!"

"What? What fire?" Eric asked frantically. "I don't see any fire ... w– where is it?"

Zak winked, and Eric caught on. All of a sudden, he began running around in panicked circles screaming his head off like Chicken Little when he claimed that the sky was falling.

"Fire! Fire! Run for your lives, ahhhhhhhhh!" Zak paused and looked his friend right in the eyes, "Dock," he said, meaning to meet him at the dock later. The guards were running toward Eric and Zak as they ducked into one of the side tunnels. He smiled. So far, everything was going according to plan. Eric winked back and continued hollering, racing in a frenzy down the passage.

"It's coming closer! Run!" Soon the group of hefty men congregating at the end of the tunnel came stampeding along in a great panic.

"Where's it comin' from?" One guy asked another.

"I dunno, but I reckon we should get out while we still got the chance!" another responded.

Just as the last man came thundering down the passageway, Zak adeptly snatched the brass key ring from his back pocket. As soon as the guards lumbered out of sight, Zak went out into the open with great satisfaction at his own skill. Zak never stopped planning, making alternate schemes in case something went wrong, and never stopped thinking, for a moment. Assuming the worst-case scenario, he thought perhaps the candlestick lever he had used earlier to unlock the floor could be locked so that it would not budge, without a key. Of course, Zak had cleverly accounted for this, hence the ring of keys swinging from his fingers. Whistling a merry tune, he walked into the large open room and stuck a key in the hole in the wall beside the candlestick lever. It did not fit. He tried a silver key. It was too small. A brass key, too large; a copper key, too wide; a gold key, too narrow. Beginning to get frustrated at this lack of success, he growled softly. Determined, he tried all the keys. Finally, the last one fit.

Zak stuck the key in the hole and turned it, nothing happened. This was the last key; if it didn't work, his whole plan was going out the window! With an angry sigh, he turned it again, trying one last time. The candles went dim and a mechanical groaning could be heard. The floor in the center of the room began to separate from the edges. It lifted up and, again, revealed a hole: a dark deep hole. Zak approached the edge, rimmed in blackness and hung on tightly with his left hand. Carefully, he lowered himself until he was hanging by his fingertips.

Letting go, Zak's arm brushed against the wall and flicked a switch that turned on a dozen round lights attached to the wall of the circular room. Zak fell a few feet and landed on a hard dirt floor. He gazed in awe at the contents of the room. Turning a full three hundred and sixty degrees, he grinned.

"This is it!" he exclaimed to himself. Pile upon pile, row upon row, stack upon stack of bullet-shaped objects filled the room. "But ... what are they?" he wondered aloud. "Missiles ...?" Suddenly, everything fit.

Enthralled by his discovery and elated that everything was coming together, Zak jogged over to the other end of the oval shaped storage room. There were several doors, each leading down an unexplored passageway. They were fitted with locks so Zak tried the keys on the guard's ring. After four or five tries, he found one that worked. The door slid silently open, revealing a large, dark, and cavernous room, even bigger than the one containing the missiles.

There was a light switch on the wall. Zak flipped it, and the room was illuminated with a soft, yellow glow. "Wow!" Standing before him was a huge jet plane! He was in such awe, that he could not think, could not move, could not do anything for several moments. He went closer to inspect the aircraft but sensed the presence of others. Suddenly, a scene flashed through his mind. Croogar and his men were tearing through the jungle, looks of hatred on their red, sweaty faces. In the distance, Zak could see a wide-open field, beneath which was "the hole," where he was poking around. Then the image went dim, as if a movie projector had been turned on in his head and then turned off again. At that moment, his gift became clear. He knew he was seeing what was occurring in the jungle, even though he could not see it with his eyes. As fast as he could, he turned off the lights and rushed out of the hangar.

Questions buzzed around in his head, possible amendments to his escape plan began forming. This airplane could be the perfect ending to his plan. If they were able to get it off the ground …

A calm but firm voice ordered, "You there, come out, now. You don't belong down here." Zak looked up at the owner of the gruff but serene voice, and his gaze traveled to his companions: six black-clothed men and Croogar.

Zak looked around and saw a small door off to his right. He pretended not to see it and hung his head low. "You're right," he admitted, playing along, "I shouldn't be down here, but it seemed so mysterious and intriguing, I couldn't help myself." As the group stood there, processing what he'd said, Zak dove for the door and threw it open, bolting it shut behind him. Luckily for him, the door led to a tunnel. Zak fumbled with his Swiss Army Knife and found the flashlight and flicked it on in an instant.

As he dashed down the narrow passage, he heard pounding on the door and then the splintering of brittle wood. The tunnel was tall enough for Zak to stand upright, but the large men behind him would have to stoop down if they wanted to chase him. Sighting a dim light at the end of the passageway, Zak ran toward it and found himself above ground, directly below the very same palm tree he had clung to only hours before. "Hmmm," Zak thought, pondering how he wound up above ground. "I guess the tunnel was sloping upward all along, and I didn't notice it." He shrugged and decided it wasn't important right then. Already he could hear the echoing voices of the men coming up the tunnel.

Zak got his bearings and sprinted off down the path toward the harbor. Past palm trees and leafy shrubs, through a swarm of gnats, Zak ran, seeing only from the dim dawn light. The sun was not fully up, but it was peeking out from around the other side of the island, evaporating the hazy mist that shrouded the jungle like a foggy cloak on a child in the winter. Finally, he approached the dock, sweat streaming down his temples and neck and looked around for Eric, who was waving from the pier. He was standing beside a boat, beckoning frantically.

"Didn't you just come from the "hole" or whatever it was you were calling it? Why are you so out of breath?"

"Yes! Croogar and his henchmen are after me! Okay?" he

exploded in his friend's face. He took a deep breath to steady himself. "They're coming after us, they're on their way, probably not far behind, and we've got to think of something. Please help me."

"Okay, did you find anything?"

"Oh, yes, I found missiles! That's what we're manufacturing here!"

"Missiles? Really? That's awesome!"

Zak looked at Eric, raising one eyebrow skeptically. "I ... mean ... that's bad?"

"Hello! What do you think they want to do with a whole load of missiles?! Probably blow some place up! That's not good!"

"Oh, right, um, anything else?"

"Yeah ..." Another scene flashed through Zak's head, much like the earlier one. The same people were in the vision, but they were heading toward the dock this time, not far away from where they stood at that moment. "I gotta tell you as we run," Zak hissed, grabbing his friend's sleeve and dragging him away.

"What? Why?" Just then, they saw Boss's men crashing through the brush.

"That's why!" Zak exclaimed, pointing. "Come on!"

They ran back along the trail. Zak's head pounded from the running, but also from the intense thinking. "How were we going to get out of here? If we could get that plane, that would be great, but who knew how to fly the darn thing."

"All right, Eric, here's what you need to do," he said, still running wildly, "round up all the kids from the Containment Center, the assembly warehouse, and that other little metal shack where they keep kids. The older kids can help you, and when you get them all, round 'em up and bring them to the hole. I'll meet you and Nick there, so let Nick know where it is and send him right away. Keep the kids calm and under control as much as possible and usher them to the hole as quickly as you can. By then, I should be back," he assured his pal, running off toward the hole.

Zak tore back through the jungle, feeling his energy running low and draining quickly. He had not had any sleep or food. How much longer could he keep going? Zak could only guess. And he could only hope it was long enough to complete the job he knew he had to do. The teen approached the hole and jumped down into it. There he waited, and soon enough, Nick appeared, eyes wide.

"Come down here!" Zak hissed, waving his arms to get the boy's attention. Nick caught sight of his friend, obeyed, and went close to Zak who was crouched in a corner.

"I've got a job for you, Nick" Zak announced, without giving him a second to prepare himself for the task. "First, thanks so much for all your help." He looked down at the ground, embarrassed at getting a little emotional in front of his friend, "I could not have done this without you. You, and everyone else, like Eric for his vision and everything. I know it must be scary, but we're going to get through this." Zak laid his hand reassuringly on Nick's shoulder. Grinning he instructed, "Now find the guards, Boss, oh and Croogar too, and lure them here to the hole." Without question or reproach, Nick nodded and took off down the path, eyes alert and watchful. Zak seized the opportunity to regroup his nerves and slumped back against the dirt wall to rest.

Meanwhile, Eric worked on transferring all the kids from the Containment Center over to the hole. He was glad he had been able to help Zak with his plan, however crazy, that was going to get them all home safely. He was not sure exactly how he knew this, but he had a feeling God was filling him with the courage and power he needed to do his part in this huge task. Now, he felt like he could conquer the world with this newfound strength.

Eric had passed on the outline of Zak's plan to the older kids so they could work together to make it happen. Sara was comforting all the younger, frightened children, and told them everything was going to be all right. "Listen," she said, pulling aside one especially disturbed little girl named Allie, "We are going to get you back to your mommy and daddy just as soon as we can. God's going to make sure of that, you hear?"

The young one sniffed, wiping her nose with the back of her hand and nodded. Sara smiled warmly and took the child's hand in hers, continuing to herd the kids in their walk to freedom.

Delilah was also doing her best to assist. She had been sent to the warehouse to collect the kids there and was single-handedly herding them in the direction of the hole. Some of the kids were weak with exhaustion from working from dawn until dusk in the factory, being on their feet all day long, with inadequate sleep and barely enough food to eat. With the aid of some of the bigger, stronger boys, she supported the weak ones, letting them lean on her as a crutch all the way to the hole. It was tiring work, but she did not mind. Delilah knew who was behind all this, and she knew deep in her heart that, just like she'd heard Sara say to console the little girl, everything was going to turn out all right. All they had to do was trust God and lean on him, as so many of the other kids were leaning on her.

While many of the other kids used their gifts in their own

individual ways, despite the toll it was taking on them, Joy did not have to make a special effort to use her gift. She had gone to the shack, where the kids were the most frightened, knowing they were on their last days, and encouraged everyone around her, giving them helpful, motivating advice, and shining her brilliant smile all around.

When they were about three quarters of the way there, Eric met up with Delilah's group. They worked together to get the children to the hole so they could all be together, like his friend wanted. Once they had achieved that, Eric doubled back to lend a hand to Joy. He arrived in the clearing where the shack was located, crawled through the hole in the sand Zak had left from his visit before, and met up with Joy. She was busy keeping the kids under control, so he helped her as they herded the frightened captives to the hole. The children followed the two like sheep following their shepherd, as they meandered along the vegetation to the clearing.

Nick finally returned, as Zak waited patiently and out of sight. Instead of joining Zak, the boy darted off into the undergrowth. Knowing the guards would soon follow, Zak climbed out of the hole and hid himself behind a palm tree laden with ripened coconuts. Sure enough, Boss arrived, red-faced and sweating up a storm, followed by not six, but twelve, cronies all with fierce and angry looks on their faces.

"Where is he?" asked Boss, turning to his men for an answer. Zak looked around and grabbed a fallen coconut. He took aim and threw it into the hole.

Hearing the rustling, one pointed angrily and cried, "Down there!"

"Don't loose you're marbles, I saw, I saw him," Boss snapped. They were all down there in a flash, all except for

Croogar that is, who was told to keep watch above ground.

"Oh, I'll take care of that old geezer later," Zak thought to himself. He pressed a hidden button, he'd discovered earlier, which put the ground back in place and pocketed the keys he'd stolen from the guards. Without those, there was no means of escape since the men couldn't fit through the exit Zak had found. He also took the time to seal the remaining escape route with logs lying near by. Croogar stood and watched helplessly, as the ground covered Boss and his henchmen.

VII. The Escape

Zak ran around the perimeter of the hole and soon located the group of frightened children hidden from view.

"We've got them all here," Eric said, "now what do we do?"

"I've discovered an airplane in a separate area of the hole. I don't know how to fly one or anything, but I think it's our only hope of getting off this island."

"Great, so what do we do?" asked Nick in exasperation. "We've got a plane but no pilot!" He said it louder than intended, and Jason overheard them.

"Did you say you need someone to fly an airplane?" he asked hopefully.

"Man, you sure do like to eavesdrop on other people's conversations, don't you?" commented Zak rather bitterly.

"Sorry." He blushed and looked away. "I just want to help."

"Leave him alone," Nick insisted, "if he can help, let's hear him out."

Zak rolled his eyes. "Fine, continue."

"Well, I'm training to get my pilot's license. I've taken all the classes and everything, it's just not legal yet. I could probably do it." His eyes were bright, his optimism and confidence contagious.

Nick looked to his friend, raising his eyebrows in question.

"What?"

"Well, what's the verdict, your honor?"

With a deep sigh, he gave in. "All right. I'll show you where it is. But after that, you're on your own. I haven't been on many airplanes, let alone flown them! Let's just hope you don't get us all killed. Keep those guys hidden over here," he instructed Nick. "I'll be back as soon as I can." He stopped, then spoke again, a new thought occurring to him. "If you get discovered, run and hide ... some place, I don't know where. Try to stick together if at all possible, and if you see or hear anything don't be seen!"

Nick nodded he understood. With that, he was off.

Jason flashed a bright grin and hurried after Zak as they made their way down into the hole. Once underground, Zak warned his friend. "We've got to act fast, okay?"

"Aye, aye captain!"

They crept as inconspicuously as possible into the airplane hangar and over to the craft itself. The ignition keys were hanging on a hook by the light switch, so Jason grabbed them and hoisted himself up to the cockpit with Zak's assistance. Soon, they were inside, and Jason was checking the controls out.

He grimaced. "What? What's wrong?" Zak asked.

"Well, it's just, I've been learning to fly small personal aircraft, commercial jets come later, and well ... these controls and things are a little different ..."

Zak sliced through his insecurity. "Can you fly this thing or not?" He fixed the boy with a steely gaze.

He gulped. "Yes, I think so."

"Good. Figure out what you need to. I'm going to see how we can get this thing up above ground. See ya!" He climbed carefully down from the cockpit and ran toward the back of the hangar. There was a gigantic metal door, like the ones where semis that carry food and other goods across the country are stored. A large red button opened the door. It creaked and rumbled as it slowly inched upward, like a garage door. Finally, the light of day shone down, and the airstrip he had found earlier stretched before him. The airstrip was paved, with lights on either side, and had dashed lines painted down the center. It looked like it stretched all the way to the edge of the island, where the ocean met the sand.

Really tired from running back and forth, here and there and everywhere, Zak jogged wearily back to Jason.

"All right, man," he said, trying to catch his breath, "the door's open for you down that way." He pointed in the direction from which he had just come. "It leads out onto an airstrip. If you can get this thing out there, I'll round up all the kids, and we may have a shot out of here!"

"Okay." The boy looked worried, unsure of his abilities, but Zak had faith in him. "Look Jason, don't worry, okay? God's going to take care of us. We just have to trust Him." The boy nodded faintly in reply. Zak had no time to stay and chat, so he headed back to where he had left everyone. There they were, talking quietly, sitting in the brush. Nick, Eric, Delilah, Joy, and Sara approached him.

"What can we do?" Sara asked.

"Yeah, how can we help?" Joy wanted to know.

"You guys, thanks so much for everything. I don't know how I'll ever repay you."

"Oh, don't mention it," Joy brushed aside the gratitude. "Besides, I've got a feeling some very angry men are probably after us right about now. Don't you think you should tell us how we're going to escape?" A smile played about her face. Although Zak had known her only a few minutes, he was already beginning to like her optimism and ability to remain calm, happy, and rational even in stressful times like these.

Zak took a deep breath to clear his mind. He had a million different thoughts bouncing around in there, and it was getting overwhelming. "Okay. Jason's out on the runway right now, waiting for us. We've got to round up all these kids and get them on the plane. The sooner, the better, because that means we can get out of here, off this island, and away from Boss and Croogar."

"Got it," Delilah affirmed. Everyone else nodded and began ushering the others in the direction Zak had indicated. Within minutes, they had successfully accomplished the task and were herding the children up the retractable steps and into the airliner. Although it was a large craft, kids shared seats and squeezed together so everyone could fit. They were making one trip and one trip only. There was no space for a return flight.

"All right everyone," Zak addressed the crowd of excited, noisy children. "Is there anyone missing? We're taking off soon, and we don't want to leave anyone behind. Look carefully to see if there is anyone we need to go out and look for." The buzz of chatter died down as kids turned left and right, looking for their friends, and those they had worked beside at the assembly warehouse.

"Anybody you've noticed?"

There was a communal, "No," and shaking of heads.

"Good–,"

"Wait! Andrew! Where's my brother Andrew?" Mary suddenly cried out from the back of the airplane. "Andrew! Are you in here?" There was no response. Everyone was looking around them, under the seats, up front, down in back, but he was nowhere to be found. Mary was becoming frantic. She jumped up from her seat, and stumbled down the aisle in search of her brother. "He's not here! Someone has to go back for him!" she cried, tears streaming from her clear blue eyes.

"Okay, calm down. We're going to find him, don't worry," Zak assured her. Turning to his companions, Zak distributed instructions. "Sara and Eric," the two fixed him with steadfast gazes, "Can you come with me and help me find Andrew? I know he's got to be here somewhere, and there's no way we are leaving anyone behind."

"I'd be honored," Eric agreed, bowing slightly.

"Yes, me too. I know I'd want Nick to come back for me if I were lost." They exchanged brief smiles, and then the three exited the aircraft.

Zak called up to Jason in the cockpit. "Wait here, ready to go. As soon as we find the boy, we'll come right back, and then we've got to hit it and get out of here, got it?"

Jason nodded obediently. Zak turned to catch up to his friends, but then paused to mention one last thing to the pilot. "If we don't make it back in time, and if Boss and Croogar find you here, go. Take off, get to the airport and keep these kids safe. Okay?"

"I'll do my best, Zak," Jason replied, worry creasing his forehead.

"I know you will, I have faith in you."

Jason smiled. "Good luck."

"Thanks."

Zak ran after Eric and Sara. "Let's split up to look for him. Eric, you go to the Containment Center, Sara the assembly station, and I'll go to the storage shack. We'll meet as soon as possible back at the assembly station, okay?"

They nodded.

"I don't know how much time we have, but I know it's very limited. We must work as quickly as possible. Break!" They ran off down the forest trail, then broke off in their different directions, as the path split accordingly.

Zak jogged down to the old metal shack, slowing down as he reached the small corrugated iron door. He opened it and peered inside. "Andrew, Andrew," he called softly as he made his way down the rows of beds. "Andrew, I'm here to take you home. Come out, if you're in here." It was dark with shadows inside the hut, and it was challenging to make out distinct objects. He could really only see shapes. With a sigh, he was just about to give up and go meet Sara and Eric when he heard a rustling sound.

"Andrew? Are you there?" Zak squinted, trying to see in the dim lighting. He walked over to the far corner where he thought he heard the noise. Behind one of the bunks in the very back corner, he discovered a tiny frightened boy, wrapped up in a protective ball. When Zak reached out a hand to touch him, reassure him, try to communicate to him that he was not going to hurt him, he flinched and shrunk back even further.

"Are you Andrew? Look, it's going to be all right. Mary is waiting for you, we all are. Don't you want to go home?"

The little boy peeked up from behind his dirty hands. His eyes were swollen and red from crying, his cheeks filthy and streaked with grime. "W– who are you?" He trembled as he spoke, fighting back tears.

"I'm Zak, and I've come to rescue you. Now, come on, we don't have much time at all."

"Where are you taking me?" Andrew asked, not fighting

the older boy, just curious.

"There is an airplane full of kids ready to take-off and get you home. They're just waiting for you." He took hold of the boy's hand and pulled him up from the sand. They walked together as quickly as possible, and Zak answered his questions.

"Really? They're waiting for me?" He looked incredulous, eyes wide, face hopeful.

"Yes, now come on." Zak's long strides doubled Andrew's tiny ones. He pulled on the little hand, trying to move more quickly. Soon, they arrived at the designated meeting spot. Eric was waiting with Sara, both wearing worried, impatient expressions on their long, lean faces.

"Zak! You made it!" cried Sara, overjoyed.

"Yeah, and I've got Andrew. Now let's go." He was all business. They nodded and set off briskly. As they made their way slowly back to the hole, where the plane was waiting, Eric stopped dead in his tracks.

"What is it?"

"Oh, I don't know, I thought I heard a noise." He looked disconcerted, pulse throbbing rapidly in his veins.

"It's probably just an animal. Come on," Sara dismissed the thought.

Several seconds later, Eric stopped again and stood silently.

"Honestly, if we keep on going like this we'll never make it there!" Sara said, exasperatedly. She tugged on Eric's sleeve. "Let's go!"

"No, wait. Listen." He perked his ears, and the others did as he commanded.

There was a distinctive crunching of twigs underfoot. "I heard that," Zak affirmed. "We've got company, come on." He pulled Andrew after him, but the little boy simply could not move any faster. After a couple of minutes, Andrew had grown tired, with insufficient food and sleep and his short legs were no match for his companion's, so Zak slung him up on his back and carried him. They trotted swiftly through the fields into the forest.

Sara stole a glance backwards and caught the movement of branches several hundred yards behind them. "They're gaining on us!" she cried.

"Don't worry about them, focus on getting to the plane," Zak instructed. She obeyed and was silent. There was still another good four or five minutes before the hole would even be visible, and the people chasing them weren't bothering to be subtle anymore. They were crashing through the forest, not too far behind them.

"We're never going to make it there in time!" Eric wailed.

"Don't say that! Keep moving!" Zak was fierce. His determination pushing them on, despite his own weariness. Just then, Croogar's face became visible behind them. His teeth were bared ferociously, like a wild animal, slobber foamed out of his mouth, flecking off as he ran.

"C'mere kid, you caused us more trouble than I ever thought possible!" He struggled to catch his breath, but the kids did not hear his next words, so intent were they on reaching the airplane. Finally, it came into view. The four crashed out of the jungle into the open field. There it was, just as they had left it. Jason had his eyes peeled and as soon as they broke through the clearing, he started the plane's engines. In several seconds, the rotors inside the engines were gaining speed and everything was warming up in preparation for take-off.

Jason motioned for them to hurry. He let down the staircase, and they began to climb up before it was fully descended. They could see Jason, in the pilot's window, mouthing at them with a frightened expression on his face.

Zak was about to climb onto the steps, reaching for the outstretched hand of Eric, when he felt a great blow to his back. He fell backwards instantly, rolling to his side, so as not to crush Andrew, saddled on his back. Croogar had lunged and hit him with impeccable accuracy. He now had Zak and little Andrew pinned to the ground.

"I've got you now! Boy, Boss'll be pleased," he snarled, eyes crazed with madness.

"Let me go!" Zak struggled to free himself, but he was no match against the determined madman. Soon Boss and the rest of his men, having escaped the other section of the hole, arrived sweaty and out of breath, but they were headed straight for the plane.

"Jason!" Zak called from the ground, "Go, go!" He waved his arms, indicating for him to leave. The boy gave him a defiant look out the window as if to say, "I'm not leaving without you." Zak shook his head vigorously. "No," he mouthed. "Go!" Jason bit his lip then turned to the controls and prepared for take-off. Boss's men were now swarming the aircraft, but the staircase was fully lifted again.

Zak did not know how he was going to get off the island, but that was not his biggest worry at the moment. The most important thing was saving as many people as possible. Besides, he knew he could find a way out.

The noises emanating from the plane's engine increased in volume and pitch. There was a brief pause then, within seconds, the craft was moving slowly down the runway. It picked up speed and zoomed away. Zak craned his neck to see the thing bounce once, then take off into the open air. Everyone watched in silence as it grew smaller and smaller, until it was just a speck in the sky. Finally, the plane was gone. Zak prayed they would make it across the ocean and to the airport safely. That was all he could do.

"You!" Boss pointed accusingly at Zak, still pinned uncomfortably underneath Croogar. "You just helped our whole work drew escape." A nasty grin spread across his thick lips. "You'll pay for this, you'll pay big," emphasizing the word "big."

Boss's men shuffled around uneasily. One particularly large one cleared his voice. "E-hem. Er, let him up." He shifted his eyes around.

Croogar looked up at the one who had spoken. He screwed his eyes up and fixed them at the man. "What did you say?"

"Er, um, I said get up off him. You's hurtin' him." This time with a bit more confidence.

Now Croogar's fuming anger was directed at the defiant member of the crew and away from Zak, still pinned underneath. "You come here! You do not talk back to your commanding officer like that! I'll show you a thing or two!" When he jumped up from the ground, reaching for the throat of the poor cadet, Zak took advantage of the opportunity. He leapt up, pulling Andrew with him. Everyone was focused on Croogar and the cadet, taking no notice of the two boys as they slunk away. Zak tried to be as inconspicuous as possible as he sprinted as lightly as a fox into the cover of the forest.

Once inside, he ran as fast as his weary legs could carry him along the beaten trail to the dock. He heard yells and angry cries from behind him, but he did not look back. As Zak neared his destination, the sound of heavy breathing and footsteps grew nearer and nearer. He knew Boss and Croogar followed by their crew were far behind.

Breathless and near exhaustion, Zak saw the boat used to bring him to the island, luckily not moored on the buoy further out in the harbor, but fastened securely to the posts supporting the dock. He sighed, weighing his options. It was clear that the craft was the only viable escape. Now that the plane had left, he had no other options. He had never driven a boat before, but he had watched closely when Croogar had done it on their way there, so he thought, "how hard could it possibly be?"

Running onto the dock, Zak helped Andrew step onto the boat deck and began to undo the mooring lines securing the craft. Croogar's furious face appeared through jungle foliage. Sweat had soaked his shirt and was pouring down his face.

"You! Boy! Stop!" he yelled, voice cracking with emotion. Zak looked up for a brief moment and moaned. The ropes were all tied in complicated fisherman's knots, unfamiliar to Zak. He struggled with the last knot, which had become particularly tight; it was not coming any looser.

"God help me!" he cried out toward the sea. Hands raw from tugging at the rope, Zak looked up once again and saw that Croogar was no less than 200 yards from the wharf. Boss and his men followed closely behind, and they all looked ready to explode.

"Come on, come on!" Zak willed the knot to come undone, but it wouldn't budge.

"Zak!" Andrew cried, pointing. "They're coming!"

"I know!" he shot back shortly, the stress getting to him.

Andrew looked away shamefully. He did not understand why Zak had responded so menacingly to him.

Just then, three heads popped up unexpectedly from the lower deck. Zak glanced up in surprise and saw that it was Sara, Eric, and Nick.

"Guys? But how did you–?"

Eric held up his hand. "No questions now. Get in."

"But–," Croogar was approaching the dock with lightning speed. Zak watched in horror as he came pounding down the rickety planks. He now had less than seventy-five yards to cover before he would reach his target.

Eric narrowed his eyes fiercely. "Just get in!" His voice was a firm command, so Zak dared not disobey. As he hopped onto the boat, Eric pushed him aside and hacked off the end of the rope with a sharp pocketknife. At last they began to drift off away from the pier. Nick stood at the steering wheel. Frantically, he tried to locate the "on" switch but could not find the ignition key.

"Oh no!" he cried, having pushed off rather hard. Now, the current was taking them out to sea. If he could not figure out how to get the boat started, then they would be in perhaps worse trouble than if they had simply remained on the island. Nick was looking around in a panic for the key, beginning to hyperventilate. At the very last possible second, Sara appeared dangling a rusty key in her fingers.

"Looking for this?" she asked nonchalantly, holding it out to him.

"Give me that!" He snatched it away from his sister, grumbling to himself as he did and got the boat started right away. In no time, they were rocketing out of the bay into the open ocean, leaving Croogar and Boss standing dumbly on the dock, yelling and waving their arms uselessly. Zak felt like laughing, but he could not bring himself to do so. Not yet, not so soon after they had been struggling in the very jaws of life.

When they were a good distance away and the island was growing smaller and smaller with each passing minute, Zak turned in awe to Nick. "W– where did you guys come from?" Sara and Eric were leaning over the railings, staring into the deep blue water. They pulled themselves away from their activity to join the others.

Nick concentrated on directing the boat and talked without straying his eyes. "Well, just before Jason was about to start down the runway, we slipped out another exit he'd discovered while he was waiting for us to come back with Andrew. It led from the cockpit straight down to the ground, so we got out really fast and ran into the forest. We ran around, staying hidden in the jungle the whole time so Boss and his men would not see us. Also, with the noise from the take-off, no one could hear us crashing through the forest, so it was perfect timing really."

"No kidding," Zak agreed.

"Anyway, then we ran to the dock, thinking that is where you would go, seeing as there was no other way you could get off the island. So we hid in the boat until you came."

"That was awesome!" Zak commended them.

"Well, thank you," Sara replied, trying to hold back a satisfied grin.

"But do you have any idea what you're doing?"

"Of course!" Nick replied. "Me and my sister have been driving boats since we were oh, seven or eight. My dad's got a speedboat over in Coronado, and we would go out whenever the weather was nice on the weekends and in the summer and stuff. We both have our boater's licences."

"Cool. Do you know where we're going though?" Zak asked, scanning their surroundings. It appeared to him that there was nothing but endless blue water for miles around.

"Yup. I've got a map right here Eric found it in the glove

compartment—along with a whole lot of other junk—and we have a compass here on the dashboard." He indicated the needle swaying slightly, but pointing in the general direction of southeast. Zak laughed.

"What's so funny?" Nick asked defensively, looking up for the first time.

"Oh, nothing. I just find it kind of ... comical that you had all that stuff, but you didn't have the key to start this thing until the last possible second!" He giggled again.

Nick grinned slightly. "Yeah, I guess that is kind of funny."

"You got enough gas?" Zak asked, suddenly concerned. "It would not be very good to have escaped, but be stranded in the middle of the ocean."

"Well, we've got about three-quarters of a tank. That should be enough to get us pretty far, but I'm not precisely sure how far it is to shore."

Eric consulted the map and then concluded, "It's about forty miles from here."

Nick looked grim. "Depending on how good the mileage this old thing gets, we may, or may not make it. We'll just have to see."

Zak nodded solemnly. There was nothing more they could do. Nick returned his attention to driving the boat, and the other three split up to think and spend some time alone in thought. Zak went to the rear of the craft, staring out past the foamy white waves created by the noisily buzzing motor. The island was completely invisible now. They were quite far away. He thought as he fixed his eyes on the water. He had been in this exact position many days ago, and his mind set had been completely different. He praised God infinitely the whole way home, just thanking Him that he had escaped the clutches of those maniac men. He knew it never would have happened without the intervention of something far greater than he was. And it had taken them all, all their abilities, their cooperation, to make it work. Zak sighed, allowing a smile to creep across his face. "God really does answer prayers. He really does care about every, seemingly insignificant little human on the Earth He created. He wasn't just some selfish, lazy power who just sat up there in Heaven." This thought calmed Zak. He knew it was really true.

Daniels left to go find a rest room and some dinner for him and his partner. Benson was left in charge. He was bored, tired, and very irritable. Mrs. Fredrickson, Mr. Fredrickson, Mr. and Mrs. Watkinson, although also quite hungry and uncomfortable, were very tired, and had no chance for escape at that moment. They huddled together, much like they had in their jail cell, in the grass. Benson looked warily over at them, but seeing that they weren't any threat, he did not bother to keep a particularly close eye on them. The foursome plotted in hushed tones together, while his attention was averted, then fell asleep, waiting for the opportune time to put their plan into action.

When Mrs. Fredrickson awoke, it was completely dark, aside from a few dim yellow streetlights casting a faint yellow circle of light around them. She glanced over and saw that Daniels and Benson were sound asleep on the park bench. She grinned, knowing this was the time. She quietly nudged everyone awake, and they stole away into the night. They made their way tiptoeing down the street. After a while, they arrived at the place they had been looking for. Mr. Fredrickson held the door open for the others, and they walked inside. Even at this late hour of night, it was bustling with activity.

At the front desk, they were greeted by the friendly police officer who had helped them locate the stolen vehicle Zak's kidnappers were suspected of using.

"Why hello Mr. and Mrs. ...?" The officer pushed back his curly locks from his forehead, biting his lip. "I'm sorry, I don't recall you surname ..."

"No problem. It's Fredrickson."

"Ah yes, and how might we help you, er, at this time of night?" The office was curious, but cheery enough.

Mr. Fredrickson's eyes glittered with excitement and anticipation. "It's related to our missing son. We think we may have a new lead ..."

The shore was coming into view. Nick glanced nervously at the fuel needle on the dashboard. It was already on empty, and they still had a little ways to go. He was not familiar with the watercraft, so he did not know how long the engine would continue to run even after it showed empty. They could only hope and pray that it would be enough.

It turned out, it was, just enough. Several hundred yards more, and they would never have made it to land. Even as Nick gradually slowed down, steering carefully until they coasted right up next to the huge dock, the engine was sputtering and complaining. But they made it.

Zak hopped off and was thrown the ropes so he could secure it to the pier. Nick turned off the ignition and assisted his sister, Eric, and Andrew off the boat. They left the boat there and went to find help.

There was a shady park looking out onto the bay where young children ran and screamed with glee. Wooden picnic benches and canopies dotted the landscape. There was a small group of adults congregating around a tall elm. The kids decided to go to them for help. If they personally could not help them, perhaps they could direct them to a telephone or police station.

As they neared, however, Zak thought he recognized some of the people talking quietly to one another. He picked up his pace. With each step, he became more and more confident that they were indeed the very people he suspected them to be. "Mom? Dad?" he called softly at first. They did not respond. He gulped and called louder this time. "Mom? Dad, is that you?" Two heads jerked up from their conversation. The looks of surprise and utter relief were unmistakable.

"Zak?" Mr. Fredrickson asked, still not believing what his eyes were telling him.

"Dad!" Zak grinned, sprinting in full force now. Within a few seconds, he reached his parents, and they joined in a big hug. "Oh, I'm so glad to see you!" Zak's voice was muffled by his father's shirtsleeve, where his head was tucked in gratefully, but they understood what he was saying.

"We've missed you so much!" Mrs. Fredrickson exclaimed, wrapping her arms even tighter around her son. Tears streamed down her face. She simply could not contain her emotions any longer. This was the greatest thing she could have asked for. Silently, she praised God for bringing her son home to safety. She knew it was His doing. She had no doubt about that.

"Mom, Dad, I can't express how happy I am to be here safe

and sound with you, but you will never believe what's happened in the past days. It's just crazy! And there are a whole bunch of kids at the airport right now–,"

Mr. Fredrickson cut his son off. "Wait, wait, wait a minute. What are you babbling about? You're safe with us here, and that's all that matters. What on earth are you talking about? Other kids? Were there other kids with you where the kidnappers were keeping you?" He gave Zak a confused look.

"I haven't got time to explain it all right now. It's a long story. Now we've got to go to them and make sure they get safely to their parents. Can you help me with that?"

Mr. Fredrickson looked to his ex-wife. They exchanged confused glances, but then Mrs. Fredrickson shrugged. "I suppose we can straighten this all out later. If you say there is something more important that needs to get done, then, well, we trust you," she smiled.

"Thanks mom. Now, what's the fastest way to the airport?"

Zak could not have been more relieved when they pulled up in the little electric golf cart driven by one of the airport officials on the boiling hot tarmac at the San Diego International airport. Everyone was exiting the plane and talking excitedly. They all knew they would see their families again soon, and they could not contain their joy.

The children were ushered off the tarmac into the cool, air-conditioned terminal. The adults and Zak gathered in a secluded corner of the room to discuss what to do with the children.

Officers Gere and Coleman arrived from San Francisco

after the Fredricksons informed them that being called off the case had been a set up. They had gladly returned to provide whatever assistance they could.

"What are we going to do with these kids?" Mr. Fredrickson asked his son.

"Yes," piped in Mrs. Fredrickson, "We don't know how to get them all home!"

"These children could have come from all over the country. There's no way we'll be able to get them to their parents!" Officer Coleman exclaimed, furrowing his eyebrows as the kids ran around him.

"Honestly!" Mrs. Fredrickson agreed. "I might be a soccer mom, and I handle the carpool bit, but this– this is too much. It's not like we can just drop them off at their houses!"

"Now wait a minute Officer," Zak said calmly. "Why don't we just ask the kids what their phone numbers are? I'm certain their parents are worried sick, and they're waiting by the phones anyway."

"Brilliant!" Officer Coleman cried. "Let's give it a whirl." The two police Officers, the Fredrickson parents, and the six kids whose help Zak had enlisted on the island aligned themselves. "All right, children," Officer Coleman addressed in a loud clear voice, "I need you all to form an orderly line in front of one of these nice people. I want you to tell them your phone number, and we'll get you home to your families as soon as possible."

Eager to return home, the kids formed several single file lines in front of the adults. Amazingly, with everyone working together to get the job done, within three hours all the guardians had been contacted and were on their way to retrieve their children. It turned out, the kids were all from somewhere in California, so depending on what part of the state they lived in, parents were hopping in their cars or booking flights down to San Diego to meet their children.

While they awaited the arrival of the parents, Zak was finally able to have a heartfelt chat with the kids he had become so close to in the past several hours.

"Everyone, I don't know what to say … how to thank you all. Joy, thanks so much for working with all those frightened little kids. I heard what you did. It was great." He looked down at the ground, nervously. "I can admit; I'm not really good with little kids, but you were awesome. Delilah, thanks for your leadership and your kindness in helping get all those kids to the hole. Jason, first of all, thanks so much for helping us make sense of Eric's dream. It helped us immensely. Second, I really don't know what we would have done if you hadn't figured out how to fly that plane! I know you'd never flown anything quite like that before. I admire your bravery, and the courage every one of you displayed out there today. Eric, thank you for sharing your vision so that we could see our way to freedom. I know you were a little scared, I think we all were, but that did not stop you from using your gift to figure out anything. And, well, we can't say that didn't benefit us in a really huge way. Sara and Nick thanks for sticking with me and not leaving me on the island to deal with those thugs. Thanks for trusting God and me, and putting your life in my hands."

As Zak fumbled with his words, he wondered silently. "How do you thank the kids that helped save your life—who trusted you and took orders from you, even though your ideas may have seemed crazy and half-baked? How to you thank kids empowered by the Holy Spirit, who were so willing to use the gifts God has blessed them with, to work together for a greater cause?" Finally, he said, "You guys ... you were great. I don't know how I'll ever repay you."

"No, Zak," Eric replied. "Thank you. You helped me find my faith. You helped me realize that I was caught up in all the minor details, but I know now that God is bigger than all of that. We aren't going to figure out every little mystery in life. Sometimes, we just have to trust that He's there and has an amazing plan for our lives. As humans, we struggle to comprehend even the smallest fraction of His ultimate plan for the universe."

"H– hmm," Eric continued, "and without your initiative and leadership, no doubt this never could have happened. We all might have been there for who knows how long, and our families probably would never have seen us again. It's you we owe big time, not the other way around."

"Yeah," piped Joy, brightly. "It was our pleasure to be a part of the plan."

The kids looked at one another appreciatively. "Well, I think it's safe to say this could not have been possible without our teamwork, trust in one another, and most importantly in God," Zak concluded with a great big smile. Everyone nodded vigorously.

As the number of waiting children became less and less, the little group, the masterminds behind the escape, conversed and exchanged contact information so they could stay in touch.

"Oh, look, there's mom!" Sara exclaimed, jumping up from the floor where she had been making a paper clip chain. She grabbed Nick by the arm, and the two made their way outside. Through the large glass windows making up the front wall, Zak watched as they ran over to the blue mini van. A tall blond lady with similar features hopped out of the car, and the three wrapped in a great big hug. They shared a few tearful words.

Zak watched from a distance, twiddling his fingers idly.

A short while later, Sara ran back inside, making her way over to Zak and threw her arms around him. "Thanks so much Zak. You saved my life."

Nick was standing rather awkwardly beside her. When his sister had finished, he grinned. "Yeah, man. Thanks. I owe ya big time."

Tired of denying it, Zak grinned. "You're very welcome. Now, go. Your mom's waiting."

They nodded, Sara's clear, intriguing eyes bright with unshed tears. The two hastened back to their mom. Sara got in the front seat of the van and, as they were pulling away, leaned out the window, waving and called back, "Bye Zak!" She wore an enormous smile of pleasure. Zak could see her lean her head down on her mother's shoulder through the back windshield of the minivan. He sighed, thankful that they were back with their mom again, whom they had so dearly missed while on Quaqilé Island. Everything was working out just find.

One-by-one, the rest of his friends were taken away, making sure to say their good byes, and making promises to stay in contact. When all the children had been picked up, there was one remaining. Finally, her parents arrived and gratefully guided her to the taxi they had come in. Just as she approached the vehicle, she turned back and waved with the hand that was not firmly entwined in her mother's. "Thank you," she mouthed.

"See ya," he replied as he plopped down in a cracked leather chair beside the wall. The girl disappeared inside the vehicle and drove off. "Well that was exhausting!" he decided. And it was, but oh so rewarding. Finally, after what seemed like an eternity, his job was done. The last child was safely returned to his parent. The mothers and fathers seemed absolutely elated to have their children back safe in their arms once again. He felt as if a huge burden had just been lifted. Now, he was free. The Lord had helped him to succeed in his task.

VIII. Arrest

After Zak explained the project Boss was heading on Quaqilé Island, Officers Coleman and Gere quickly summoned-up a SWAT team, and they all took a jet back to the island. Zak was a bit wary to return to the place where he had been treated so poorly, plucked from his home, kept from his family, made to work under harsh conditions, and nearly killed. But eventually, he was convinced that was not going to happen again, and his assistance would really be helpful.

As soon as the airliner came to a screeching stop on the runway, the police force disembarked and spread out to search for their targets.

Croogar caught sight of the uniformed cops and panic seized him. His automatic instinct was to run, to try to escape. So he tried running out one of the tunnels leading from the hole, but they were still blocked from earlier.

"Shoot!" Zak heard the man hiss. He continued to try to find a way out, but there was simply no way. He was completely surrounded. Finally, he gave up.

Officer Coleman approached the man, looking down into the huge depression in the ground.

"You have the right to remain silent. Anything you say, can and will be used against you in a court of law," he finished reading Croogar his rights and then led the extremely unhappy man to the plane.

"But– but I didn't–,"

"Save it for the judge, buddy." Officer Coleman had had enough, he was all business and nothing Croogar said was going to convince him of anything at that moment.

Croogar set his jaw tight and narrowed his eyes angrily as he slumped off with the officer.

"Come with me," Zak commanded, showing the officers to the place where he knew the other scoundrels were located. Inside a section of the hole set deeper in the ground, the place where all the bombs were being kept, the enraged men scowled irately at the stern, armed officers as they surrounded them.

As a last ditch attempt for freedom, the Boss and his men climbed out of the depression in the ground and made a break for the harbor. But a policeman snagged the Boss immediately, throwing him to the ground so he could go after another. Soon enough, all twelve were handcuffed and secured to their seats inside the plane.

"All right everyone," Coleman addressed the Watkinsons and the Fredricksons, "we're goin' home!" The response of the delighted families sent a flock of exotic birds fleeing from their perches in the nearby trees. The commotion mixed with the frantic fluttering of hundreds of pairs of brightly colored wings as the birds flew off in a huff.

In no time at all, they were flying smoothly through the air. Zak at last was able to relax. His job was done now. The evildoers were going to their rightful place, and everyone was safe with their families. The boy was even able to enjoy the flight, pointing excitedly to fishing boats and oil tankers below, gazing in awe at the view, chatting to his mother and father.

Zak was sitting on his bed, doing his Algebra homework when he heard a knock on the door. He set the book aside and raced out of his room, slipping on his socked feet as he slid across the polished hardwood floor.

"I think I know who that is," he said with a grin to his mother as he passed by the kitchen on his way to the door. Mrs. Fredrickson looked up from her vegetable chopping, and wiping her hands on her apron, accompanied her son to greet their guests. Zak turned the knob on the door with a broad smile. "Come on in," he invited warmly showing Officer Coleman, Officer Gere, the Boss along with Croogar (who were in handcuffs), Eric, Sara, Nick, and finally Professor Feburshin to the family room.

Back at the station in San Francisco, between the time Zak returned from the island to the meeting they were having that day, Officers Gere and Coleman had not given up trying to dig up more information on Zak's case. They had been in contact with Zak who was able to provide them with more valuable information. With that help, they had located a professor who they thought may be advantageous to them. After calling him up and requesting his skills and knowledge, he agreed to make an appearance at their meeting.

The elderly man with a mop of white hair, wearing large, rectangular glasses, decked out in a lab coat and black slacks, approached Zak to introduce himself. "Hello, I'm Professor Feburshin. I work with Scientific Research and Development for Explosives. I have been requested to come be of whatever assistance I can regarding this case, since I have been informed it has something to do with bombs." His crinkly eyes twinkled. "They happen to be my specialty." He had an accent, Swedish, or German, or something like that, Zak thought.

"Pleasure to meet you Mr ... What did you say your name was?" Zak asked, rather embarrassed.

"Fe-bur-shin," the kindly man replied, breaking it down into syllables.

"Okay, great."

"It's really okay. Many people mess it up. You'll get it." Dr. Feburshin ruffled the boy's hair affectionately. "You know kid, I like you already."

Mr. Fredrickson arose from the love seat and folded up the newspaper he had been absorbed in for the past hour. Everyone exchanged greetings, firm handshakes, and found seats.

"We all know why we are here, but I'll recap," Officer Coleman began. "As you know, Jake," he said sternly, shifting his glance to the fidgety man Zak had known as "Boss," "you have committed a huge, colossal–," he paused searching for words, "… very serious, to say the least, crime and you will serve your time in jail accordingly." Jake nodded begrudgingly. "I just want ... an explanation, something to justify all the things you have done! How did this all come to be? How did you organize such an elaborate scheme? Surely you couldn't have done it all on your own, you must have had at least some outside help, did you not?"

Everyone turned to Jake and fixed their eyes on the pitiful and disheveled man. He took a big breath and started his explanation. "You've got me now. I might as well just tell you everything–,"

Officer Gere butted in with a snide grin, "Yes, you had better do just that! And I mean everything. You will gain nothing from withholding information from us, in fact, it will only be to your detriment."

Annoyed, Jake continued as if he had not been interrupted, "I was brought up Christian, and my folks were very strict. They were what most people called 'extremists.' We did the usual, ya know, go to church, read the Bible, pray. But my parents took everything to the extreme. We weren't allowed to do anything fun, or even play with other kids, especially non-Christians. My dad had this insane notion that if we mingled with them, we'd be contaminated, or something, turn out just like 'em: heathens and what not. My little sister and I studied the Bible day and night and sat in church for hours on end. We didn't like it, but there was nothing we could do. To protest or stand up to my father was–," he shook his head, the memories clouding his eyes, and looked down at the floor. With a steadying breath, he continued, "–a big no-no. You just didn't cross into that dangerous territory. As I grew up, I began to understand what it really meant to be a Christian—that it wasn't about just reading the Bible. It was about forming a relationship with God, about serving him and devoting my life to him."

There he scoffed, "Don't know why I ever fell for that … it's lies, deception, all of it! But anytime I did something wrong—even one tiny little mistake—I was punished, severely, either whipped or beaten or isolated or even starved. I learned to hate Christianity when I probably should have been mad at my parents. But anyway, I began to hate everything about God. I learned to hate it with a passion. I think I got carried away and … most certainly went over the edge."

"When I was fourteen, I had had enough. I couldn't bear it any longer. So, being the coward that I am, I abandoned my sister and ran away from home to live on the streets. Croogar here took me under his wing and got me into the drug dealing business so I could earn a living. Before I knew it, I had formed this brilliant plan to rid the world of the most controlling, stuck-up, self-righteous group on Earth: Christians. Yes," he said when everyone displayed looks of disbelief on their faces, "I was going to wipe them all out ... completely. Once I had done that, I had plans, extraordinary plans, for bigger and better things. I thought, if the Christians were gone, then my problems would decay, just like their bodies."

"What plans could be bigger than that?" Zak asked, still astounded that someone would actually try to do such a monstrous thing.

Ignoring his question, Jake kept right on going with his life story. "My father was the president of a company called Scientific Research and Development of Explosives. His business did research about missiles and bombs to enable them to do good and productive things, like creating underground holes for subways, you know stuff like that. These explosives were much more accurate, than say, dynamite for instance, because they could be programmed to blow up in certain formations and in certain areas."

"I stole my father's blueprints for the latest missile they were designing. My plan was to build not just one, but hundreds of them. I'd program the missiles to hit certain churches and highly populated Christian areas all over the world." Jake sighed and looked to the embroidered carpet at his feet.

"So, so you just wanted to kill them?" Officer Gere asked, dumfounded. "That has a name, it's a thing we like to call genocide," she added dryly.

Jake nodded. "I thought, you know, if I exterminated 'em,

all my problems would ... poof ... disappear along with 'em."

"Well, you were wrong! It's a good thing you never actually got around to putting your plan into action, or else ..." Mrs. Fredrickson gulped; everyone knew what she meant by "or else."

"Yeah, I suppose you're right."

"Okay, we've got the picture now, but how do we tie into this?" Eric asked, "Why'd ya have to kidnap us, huh?"

Jake could hardly bear to make eye contact with the innocent boy who was asking the same question he was asking himself. Although he knew what his intentions once were, he no longer felt the same passion to destroy and conquer. "Do you remember working in the warehouse?" he queried.

"Do I remember? Do I remember?! How could I forget that gruesome place?" he shot back.

Wincing, Jake said, "Well, all that time you were assembling bits and pieces of missiles. I didn't let you build the whole thing because otherwise you would have discovered what you were making, you know, gotten smart on us. But I guess it didn't really do that much good anyhow because that boy figured it out all on his own, despite all the precautions I took."

"But what about Mr. Coonfeld? You were involved with his murder, were you not?" Zak asked accusingly.

Croogar spoke up for the first time since he had entered the room and strayed from his taciturn personality. "We was both involved. We killed him ourselves, the both of us."

"B– but why?"

"We had to, see, 'cause he knew too much," Croogar replied defensively. "He knew a little about our plan, and we couldn't risk him spillin' the beans. Coonfeld worked with Jake's father a' the research center and 'e decided to find out who stole them missin' blue prints. We had no choice. When Zak started snoopin' 'round, we tried to' confuse 'em, make 'em think that the dog went mad an' killed him. Din' think it'd be too hard. The dog looked vicious 'nough …" he shifted his gaze and fidgeted uncomfortably.

"Wait!" Zak shouted, to everyone's surprise springing to his feet as if he had just sat on a tack. "I think I've got the rest of it all figured out! Coonfeld was a scientist, wasn't he Jake?" asked Zak, narrowing his eyes. Jake nodded indifferently as the boy continued on, voice cracking and eyes dazzling with excitement. They were like polished gems, glittering in the afternoon sunlight, gleaming with extraordinary brilliancy. He suddenly whipped around to face Feburshin. "He was a scientist who worked with Jake's dad, and he must have had a lead as to who had stolen the blueprints! You work at the same place Jake's dad and Mr. Coonfeld worked, right?" The scientist nodded. "So Jake and Croogar, they killed him."

Feburshin pointed out, "Well, they've told us that much already … what's your point?"

"Okay, okay, let me continue. Then, when I started having dreams and investigating, they had to kidnap me too to hide the evidence. They also kidnapped Christian kids from all up and down the California coast because that would keep the authorities hands' full. If the police did somehow get a tip as to what the project was that Jake was working on, they would disregard it, because they would have been too busy trying to find all the missing kids. In addition," Zak said, incorporating extortive hand gestures and facial expressions as he spoke, "they needed people to assemble the missiles."

"Why couldn't they get machines to do that for them?" Mr. Fredrickson asked.

"Because, first of all, the whole thing would have to be set up temporarily, you know, they did not want to have a whole permanent place; they wanted to be able to tear it all down when they were finished to destroy the evidence. And secondly, they would have to fill out a bunch of official paperwork from the government and everything and then they would have had to reveal the purpose of the machines. Also, they would have had to hire a company to construct everything. They would have also had to explain what they needed those resources for and the government certainly wouldn't allow that. So, they kidnapped Christian kids so that it would be like killing three birds with one stone. They would have the police out of their hair, they would have manufacturers and assemblers for their missiles, and then they could just do away with the kids when they were through!"

"Brilliant! Absolutely brilliant!" Dr. Feburshin exclaimed. "You figured it all out Zak, and now we can put these thugs in their rightful place: behind bars."

"We know now that was all wrong. I can't believe I ever agreed to do the whole thing. I mean, what was we thinkin'?" Croogar muttered to himself, staring down at his hands fidgeting uncomfortably in his lap.

"Yeah," Jake added. "If I could take it all back, I would. This was a terrible thing to even contemplate doing. Just because one man ruined my life with religion, doesn't mean I have to destroy the lives of every other follower. 'An eye for an eye makes the whole world blind.'" He shook his head sullenly, appearing sincerely sorry. "If there were anything we could do to make it right, I'd be the first to volunteer."

Zak felt triumphant and the signs of a smile played about his face, but he stopped before it could come out of hiding and show itself. Croogar and Jake looked as if their souls were being wrenched out of them and being trampled upon right in front of their faces. "No ..." Zak murmured pityingly, a shadow falling on his eyes and contorting his face. "No ... n– not jail. I– it's not the proper place for them. I– I have a better idea."

"Zak," the doctor said as if telling a small child that their mother or father had died but everything would still be fine, "they have to go to jail. They committed a very serious crime. You know that. We have no choice."

"No!" Zak objected stubbornly. "Will you just listen to my idea?"

Feburshin sighed doubtfully and agreed. "All right, go ahead."

"C– can't they reconcile with God and use their experiences to minister to unbelievers? They would be so good at it!" he insisted. With the doctor still looking skeptical, Zak continued, "I can see it in their eyes, Dr. Feburshin. They didn't mean to harm so many children. Didn't you listen to Jake? Didn't you hear what a horrible childhood he had to endure? We can't place all the blame on these two men. In a way, I believe there are many others who contributed to Jake's motivation to carry out such a deed, his parents, for example. How about giving them a test period at a school in ... say, the ghetto area where the crime rate is off the charts and people are living lives not fit for words to even begin to describe. If they exhibit signs of further malice, then by all means, you are more than welcome to put them in jail. If, however, they improve and can prove to you that they are changed men, they should be set free with their punishment being only that they have to perform community service, say maybe one form being to spread the Bible to others."

The German doctor seriously considered the suggestion but shook his head sadly. "No, I just cannot do it. Their crimes are too great."

"But– but–," Zak was near tears. Jail was not where those two belonged. Yes, he acknowledged that they had done something very wrong, but he also knew from his dreams how terrible Jake's life had been, and he could see how sorry they were for committing such a crime. The only thing prison would do was harden their hearts. That was not what they needed. They needed a loving, nurturing environment where they could grow in Christ and where they could establish a sound relationship with him. Jail was most certainly not the place for that, Zak was sure of it.

Looking at the two captives, heads hung in shame, eyes glazed with sorrow, Mr. Fredrickson spoke up. "Perhaps I can see what I can do. I'm sure the lawyers at my firm would be understanding or, at least, willing to hear my son out. After all, I am known to be a pretty convincing lawyer ..." he prided himself, grinning as he tousled Zak's hair. Zak smiled.

Zak did keep in contact with Eric, Nick, Delilah, Jason, Joy, and Sara, just like he promised. After all, he really was a man of his word. They even met up every now and again, and one time in particular not too long after the whole kidnapping incident and the proper dealings with Jake and Croogar were completed, to discuss in detail what had happened.

One thing some of the other kids wanted to know was how Zak's parents and the police officers had found them, and so quickly.

Zak explained the whole story.

"Wow!" Eric exclaimed. Everyone shared in his reaction.

"You're really something, you know that?" asked Jason. "You figured out everything. Way to go!"

"Like you said before," Delilah mentioned confidently, tossing her long auburn hair over her shoulder and fixing the whole group with a killer smile, "we couldn't have done it without using all our gifts to work together and relying on the Big Guy Upstairs."

"I still agree with that one hundred percent," Nick seconded. Everyone nodded.

"Okay," Zak said, rising from the picnic bench they were seated at, "who wants to have some fun?" Everyone voiced their approval, and they spread out on the field for a competitive game of ultimate Frisbee.

At home, things were better now between his mother and father, partly, Zak thought, as a result of the life-altering incident that forced them back together again, to work together, to function as a team, and to support each other. They saw each other about once every two weeks or so and got together sometimes on the weekends for breakfast, to take a bike ride, or just hang out. There was talk that Mr. Fredrickson might move back with them, maybe not in the same house, but in the same city at least. It was a definite improvement, and Zak had high hopes for the future. Mrs. Fredrickson was now very successful with her job and seemed to be happier, more at ease, more free.

Zak also thought often about his gift, how he was going to develop it, mold it, use it for the glory of his Lord, talk to his friends about their gifts. He now knew everybody had one; they just had to search for it. He thought about the people he had met back on Quaqilé Island: about Croogar and the Boss and the children. He thought of what might have happened, had certain forces, beyond what we as humans can comprehend, not taken action, placing Zak in the right place at the right time. For now, Zak thought, "I think there are going to be some things I just don't understand, and I'm just going to have to accept that. Because one day, it will all be revealed to me, it will all come together and make sense. But for now, I think I just have to take things one day at a time and do my very best in everything I do. That's all I can do."

If anything can be said, one thing is sure. More than one person was changed because of a young boy and his faith; more than one life was altered for the better forever; more than one person was able to change the world. It makes you wonder, what can you do?